EBONY MAKEPEACE IS DEAD

BRAD CULLEY MYSTERIES BOOK 1

JANEEN ANN O'CONNELL

ACKNOWLEDGMENTS

Much thanks to my Alpha Reader, Denise Wood, and
Beta Readers: Ally Britnell and Diana McGlinn

1

———

THE SHOOTER

She hunched over the table. Her long, dark, dank hair formed a curtain around the sides of her face. She wrote furtively, checking every few minutes to see if anyone was watching. I caught her eye; a glimpse of despair emanated from the wide, brown spheres. She turned away from my gaze. Head down, hunched over her secret, she kept writing.

I sauntered over to the table and sat down opposite her. She smelled of musk, a pleasant musk, not mouldy or stale as I had imagined. Her clothes, although dated and worn, were clean. She was writing with a pencil so badly chewed on the end, that the lead protruded through the ragged pieces of wood. Her fists clenched and her knuckles whitened. She kept writing. Her head was so low over her work, that the hair curtain now covered the front of her face.

I cleared my throat. 'Nice bit of rain we are having.'

She ignored me. It wasn't the ignoring that stunk of arrogance; it was different, as if she didn't hear me. I sat for a few more minutes watching her, her head almost resting on the table.

I'd watched her come to this café most mornings

I

for two weeks. The café had a nice ambience, not my scene. I am a trendy fellow, and this place was, well, mundane. There was nothing about its décor to set it apart from any other café on a suburban strip. But something drew her to it. The staff perhaps?

With my right hand, I reached into my jacket and slid the small gun out from its hiding place. Resting it on my lap, I touched the tip to make sure the silencer was still attached. I would wait for the right moment.

This was the second time I'd been told to kill someone. She was my target. The instructions were brief, but clear. I was expected to point the gun that hid on my lap at her abdomen, pull the trigger, put the gun back in my jacket, and walk away.

The security cameras would record me approaching her table, would watch as I attempted small talk and would take no heed when I got up from the table to leave. They would not identify me because my disguise had me looking so ordinary, no one would look twice. But this was conjecture, I hadn't pulled the trigger yet. She raised her head and stared through my disguise into my soul.

'Why do you think you can encroach on my space?' she hissed. 'I am using every ounce of strength I can muster to prevent myself from leaning over the table and slapping your smug, superior expression. Go away, leave me alone.'

The menace she tried to force into her voice struggled to find its way out. Instead, she was left with a rasp that bordered on a whisper. Her intent was clear, however: she wanted me away from her, to leave her alone. But that was not for her to say.

'I don't know what you have done,' I whispered across the table. 'You may not know either, but you have pissed off someone powerful. Don't speak. Listen.'

A glimmer of fear washed over her face, and she nodded ever so slightly.

'Under the table, I have a loaded gun fitted with a silencer, pointed at your abdomen. You should have started bleeding three minutes ago.'

She frowned; confusion burrowed its way into her eyes.

'The only way you will live is to pretend you are dead. I am going to shoot you. I won't shoot to kill, but I do have to shoot you. I'm going to smile at you, a nasty, vindictive, self-satisfied smile, and when I get up to walk away, you will drop your head to the table. If you're unnoticed, fall off the chair onto the floor. Chaos will ensue. They will call an ambulance. If you are not unconscious, pretend to be. When my employers look over the camera footage, they will see I've done my job and you've collapsed on the floor, presumed dead. Or, at the very least, dying. If you don't follow my instructions, we will both die.

'I will organise your death.' I raised my index fingers and indicated quotation marks around the word death. 'Just do as I say. You will see me soon.'

She stared into my very being.

I squeezed the trigger.

2

EBONY

Ebony Makepeace lay prone on the ambulance stretcher, eyes closed, breathing shallow. A paramedic used scissors to cut open her shirt and her jeans. It annoyed her; the jeans were from an op shop and the only pair she had found that fitted comfortably. Should I be worrying about my clothes? she wondered. How badly am I hurt? As the question was about to form itself into words, a paramedic clamped an oxygen mask onto her face, stifling her attempt to communicate.

'It's going to be all right,' the paramedic soothed while attaching a blood pressure pad to her arm and an oxygen reader to her finger.

'I don't believe you,' Ebony whispered into the oxygen mask. 'You are frowning and look worried.' Then darkness swallowed her consciousness.

—

'Welcome back.' The woman's voice startled Ebony, and she turned her head quickly to the side to see who was speaking.

'It's okay. You are safe. You're in Recovery. You've had surgery, and the bullet has been removed. No damage to internal organs. Very lucky girl. We'll take you to your room shortly. The police are waiting to speak to you.' The woman smiled at Ebony, then turned her attention to someone else.

While the bed was being wheeled out of Recovery and to a room, Ebony tried to focus on what had happened to her. Thoughts and images swirled around in her mind like clothes in a washing machine. She couldn't pick one item to concentrate on. They all cluttered her head, scrambling for attention. With the bed in place in the room, the equipment designed to monitor her condition plugged in and set up, and the pain meds flowing through the IV, Ebony was left to her imaginings.

It was difficult to keep her eyes open, and when through half-closed lids she saw two people walk in, police detectives by their cocky stance and boring clothes, Ebony feigned sleep. There was nothing to say to the police that they would believe. The ramblings of the man who shot her made little sense; how could she relay them to anyone else?

'Is she sleeping or drugged?' the male detective asked his colleague.

'Let's see,' the woman offered. 'Miss Makepeace, Miss Makepeace. We would like to talk to you.'

Panic seeped into Ebony's being. She wasn't a good liar, and the truth was unbelievable. The effort to lie still, to not yell at the police to leave her alone, exhausted her. Ebony gave in to the pain-killing drugs that drip, dripped from the blue square machine next to her into the canula in her hand, and hoped the detectives would take the hint.

———

'Would you like a sandwich, Ebony? Do you feel well enough to eat something?'

There were four people in her life who spoke her name, and this woman was not one of them. Ebony's eyes focussed on the nurse who was checking, adjusting, and fussing over the automated drug machine next to Ebony's bed.

'Yes, please.'

She thanked the nurse, who placed a sandwich cut into four triangles on the tray alongside her, and raised the back of the bed so she was sitting up enough to eat.

'You're welcome, dear. The bell is right next to your hand. Press it if you need anything.'

With her right hand, Ebony reached out for the plate with the sandwich on it. She wasn't hungry, but had agreed to eat, thinking she might need her strength. The ham, cheese, and tomato sandwich stayed uneaten on the plate. Ebony had been a vegetarian all her adult life and was not about to eat a sandwich with ham in it for any reason.

Putting her head back on the pillow, she tried to work through the events that had led to this moment.

———

The café, usually quiet on a Tuesday morning, had brimmed with chatter coming from groups of people ensconced on the benches, arms around each other or spread on the tables. It annoyed her. Why couldn't they find another café? She came to this one because it was quiet from Monday to Thursday. Even the music had changed. The speakers in the corners, hanging precariously from the ceiling on little hooks, whispered gentle melodies on other days— great music to have in the background while she wrote. Today's music was straight from a mainstream, cookie cutter radio station.

Standing for a moment, Ebony grappled with the thought of leaving and finding another place.

'Good morning. Let me show you to a table.' The waitress with the ivory skin, coal black hair, and deep green eyes led Ebony to a small table in the far corner of the café. 'There are only two chairs,' she said as she handed Ebony the menu. 'Put your coat on the back of that one so you'll be left alone.'

'Why is it so busy today?'

'University students passing through on the way to a conference of some sort.' The waitress pulled a pen and notepad out of her apron pocket. 'The boss is pleased. Even if we are not.'

'I'm not pleased,' added Ebony. 'I come here because it's quiet.'

'Ignore them and concentrate on your writing. They'll leave soon enough.'

Ebony thanked the girl, who must've been in her early twenties, and ordered a cheese toasty and flat white.

She'd finished her toasty and the last dregs of the flat white pooled in the bottom of the coffee cup, when the man ignored her coat and sat on the chair opposite. The fake tan on his face and hands was a shade too dark for his complexion, and the light brown beard speckled with grey covering his cheeks and chin needed a trim. *Is it real?*

He wore casual clothes that looked tailor made,

and his expensive brand name sports shoes had the "just out of the box" look. She glared at him when he spoke, hissed in his face that he had no right to bother her and to go away. He didn't go away. What was he talking about that she had pissed off someone important? Why did he *have* to shoot her?

———

Ebony had a restless night. The events of Tuesday morning, the pain in her side from the surgery, and the fear of "why me" played with her psyche, daring sleep to envelop her. With her eyes closed, going over the events in the café again, trying to recall every little detail, she did not hear the detectives come in.

'Miss Makepeace,' a female voice shrilled. 'We must speak with you.'

Ebony was used to working out problems in her head, but most of the ones she grappled with were fictitious, part of her story writing process. Should she acknowledge them and answer their questions vaguely? Or should she ignore them and pretend to sleep?

She opted for the answer behind box number one —knowing they would keep coming back until she spoke to them. Ebony opened her eyes slowly, as if she were waking from a long sleep.

'Who are you?'

'Hello Miss Makepeace. I am Detective Sanderson, and this is Detective Tomy,' the officer said, waving to the woman standing at the end of the bed. 'Her name is pronounced *toe me* for future refence.' He smirked at the woman. 'We want to chat about the shooting.'

'All right,' Ebony said. She did not need to sound feeble or vulnerable. Her voice was raspy and her throat sore. The breathing tube from the anaesthetic, she acknowledged to herself.

With the forced smile of someone who had been told to be more affable, Detective Sanderson began. 'Who shot you?'

'I don't know.'

'Had you seen him before?'

'No. How do you know it was a him?' Ebony added for dramatic effect.

'The closed-circuit camera footage,' Detective Tomy said.

Ebony nodded. She remembered the shooter telling her about the camera.

'Why would anyone want to shoot you?' Detective Tomy had a pen poised over an open notebook.

'I don't know. I don't know who it was. I don't know why he shot me. I was writing, minding my own business like I do every time I go to the café.' Ebony raised her raspy voice, deliberately adding anxiety to its timbre. As if on cue, a nurse came into the room and suggested the detectives come back another day.

Detective Tomy frowned at Ebony and let a drip of malice seep from the side of her mouth. Ebony shivered.

'Have a rest, Ebony,' the nurse said. 'I'll come back soon and help you into the shower. You'll feel better.'

———

Dinner was a plate of sausages, mashed potatoes, pumpkin, and peas, smothered with what Ebony assumed was gravy. She wasn't hungry until the smell reached her nostrils. 'But I am still not hungry enough to eat sausages,' she mumbled while moving them to one side of the plate with the fork. She ate most of the vegetables, pushed the tray away, and put her head back on the pillow. Ebony started planning her escape.

He snuck in like the detectives had. She hadn't heard him and didn't know he was there until he cleared his throat.

Startled, Ebony pulled the covers over herself and demanded to know who he was.

'It must be a good disguise if you don't recognise me,' Café Man said. 'Or are you still woozy from the drugs?'

'Both,' Ebony snarled through gritted teeth. Her heart raced with the panic that he'd come to finish her off, and she fumbled around for the button to call the nurse.

'I've moved that out of your reach. Time to kick up the plan to the next stage,' he said as he took a syringe out of his pocket and moved towards the IV line that led to the canula in Ebony's hand.

'Stop!' she tried to yell as the world disappeared around her.

Café Man melted into the hallway as the monitors attached to Ebony squealed with the alarm that she was dead.

After fruitless attempts to revive her, Ebony was covered with a sheet and moved to the hospital morgue.

Café Man, disguised as a morgue attendant, helped with the moving of Ebony's body into the refrigerated locker allocated to her. Paperwork signed,

Café Man waited anxiously for the room to empty. Ebony would have to be revived in the next few minutes.

Sliding her out of the locker, Café Man took Ebony's arm out from under the sheet and pressed a syringe into her skin.

She took longer to arouse than he was led to believe, and panic—panic that he had not felt since his father called him after he had "killed" his brother—coursed through his heart.

As Ebony's eyes focussed, her body shook and her teeth chattered.

'Why am I so cold?' she asked whoever was there.

'Shock,' said a voice she knew.

Ebony sat up. It took a few moments for her to realise where she was. 'What have you done?' The terror Ebony felt in her gut made its way out into the world.

'Saved your life by killing you. I've filled in the paperwork.'

'What? What are you talking about? I don't understand. Why am I here? How will this all pan out when they realise there is no body?'

Ebony still shivered.

Am I cold, terrified, or both?

'There will be a body. I will fill in the gaps later. Get dressed. I took the liberty of getting some clothes from your apartment.'

While she was trying to process the events that led to her being on a slab in the morgue, the comment that infuriated her the most, was the one about him being in her apartment.

'How did you get into my apartment? Who do you think you are?'

'I've told you. I am your saviour. Now get dressed.'

Café Man turned around to give Ebony some privacy. 'Let me know if you need any help,' he said to the door.

'Not likely.'

Hands shaking, Ebony managed to put on her undies by leaning against the table her body had been on. She struggled with the tracksuit pants but was grateful Café Man hadn't brought jeans. She couldn't put on her socks, so she slipped her feet into her runners without them. She asked Café Man to do up the laces.

'I thought you said not likely,' he mocked while tying them.

He handed her a bag and told her to look inside. There was a brunette wig, sunglasses, and liquid foundation in a tube.

'What's with the makeup?'

'Your skin is naturally pale, and you look even paler now. That will put some colour in your face. I'll wait while you put it on. The bathroom is over in the corner.'

'You are going to a lot of trouble,' Ebony said while Café Man opened the morgue door and led her into the hallway. 'Why?'

'Am I? I shot you. I was told to kill you. I chose not to.'

Ebony moved slowly down the hallway to the elevator, wondering how she was going to get out of the hospital without raising suspicion. Even with the disguise, she knew she looked like a patient. But what troubled her most about her situation was not her condition. It was that she sub-consciously, or otherwise, had followed the lead of the man who had shot her.

As if he'd read her thoughts, Café Man said, 'We'll get out on level three. You will sit on a seat near the elevator, and I will get a wheelchair.'

Relief swept over Ebony like waves lapping the shore.

3

——————

EBONY

Café Man parked in the laneway behind Ebony's apartment complex and helped her out of the passenger seat. He supported her while they went up two flights of stairs, every step a struggle. Ebony was grateful she lived in a low-rise building.

'You can go now. Thanks.' Ebony didn't look at him. She wanted to pretend he wasn't there. If she ignored him, he might go away.

'Are you sure? I'm happy to help. I'll make a cup of coffee or tea, whatever you prefer.'

'I don't want you to help me. You've helped me enough. I'd prefer it if you left.'

Although not feeling as forceful as she wanted to sound, Ebony stood with her feet apart, one hand on her hip. The other hand rested on the side of her abdomen.

Café Man took a business card out of his jacket pocket and handed it to Ebony. 'In case you need something. Because you are dead, you might need my help. Don't leave this apartment without telling me.' He bowed slightly at Ebony then jumped down the stairs three at a time.

Fear ran down Ebony's arm to her shaking hand while she tried to put the key in the door. The rattle of the key entering the lock echoed down the empty hallway. Keeping her head down, she peered through the hair that fell along the sides of her face. Was anyone around? She turned the key and stepped into her apartment. Leaning against the closed door, she breathed slowly, deeply, willing herself to calm down. With her hands still shaking, she locked the door behind her and made her way to the bedroom. The room was tucked away at the back of the apartment as if an afterthought. It had no windows, and as she organised herself for a shower, she wondered why the windowless room hadn't bothered her before.

The dressing on her wound was waterproof, but while she stood under the steaming, cleansing water in her own shower, Ebony wondered when she should change it. She didn't even have a general practitioner, the worst illness she ever had was the flu, and she managed that herself with Echinacea, Eucalyptus, and paracetamol. Ah, paracetamol. She would take two tablets with a cup of tea.

Dressed in loose fitting tracksuit pants and a hoodie that was too big for her, Ebony made a cup of tea and sat on the couch to drink it while mulling over her situation. She took the two pain killers. Her feet were in her slippers, socks absent. She couldn't put a sock on her left foot because of the pain from the surgery.

She fired up her laptop and learnt that alcohol wipes would keep her wound clean, and non-waterproof dressings would help it breathe. She could change the dressing morning and night. The pharmacy would have everything she needed, including more paracetamol. She didn't want Café Man in her life, but he was the only one who could get the supplies for her. She took the business card he gave her off the table where she'd thrown it and sent him a text outlining the things she needed.

His instant response was a curt, 'Sure.'

While Ebony rested her head on the back of the couch, she went through the events of Tuesday morning again. The man who sat opposite her was a total stranger. Why was he sent to kill her? Should she put any credence in his story? Of course, she should. She was nursing a 10cm incision on her left side. He killed her, then brought her back to life.

Ebony kept to herself. She had two close friends and wrote books for a living. She didn't work in an office where she could offend anyone, and communicated with her publisher via email. She saw her parents once a year at Christmas. She was an only child.

The clouds that had threatened to spill their watery contents when Ebony was leaving the hospital finally gave way under the weight and unleashed a downpour, which she was pleased to view from inside her cosy apartment. Rain lashed the living room window and blocked out the view of the park opposite the building.

The weather is reflecting my life,' she thought. Horrible.'

A gasp of realisation hit Ebony while she watched the rain; he'd told her she would have to leave this apartment, to live somewhere else. She was dead.

The cup of tea went cold while Ebony struggled to put the pieces of her life into order. Café Man had decided not to kill her. Why? It wasn't her ravishing, good looks. She deliberately played down her best fea-tures by keeping her hair untidy and her clothes unre-markable. Why was she even on his list?

Taking a sip of the tea, Ebony's mind went back to a time at the café when they had put cold coffee in front of her.

'Oh my god!' A jolt of horror ran through Ebony's body. She jumped up, spilling the tea on her leg and a cushion. 'Shit. Shit. Shit.'

Ignoring the spilt tea, Ebony hurried into the bed-room, searching for her notebook. Paranoia — she wrote about it in her novels — she enjoyed watching her characters panic and drop their bundle when they thought someone was after them. But this time it was real; a killer was after her. He'd jumped from a page in her notebook, the one she'd left behind at the café. She had to retrieve it; her latest book was in those pages.

———

Darkness enveloped Ebony's soul when she slunk down under the covers on her bed. Sleep would evade her, as it did when she was planning some disaster for a character in a story. The plan that would keep her awake tonight wasn't a new book, it was her escape.

———

'In the movies, people cut their own hair with no drama,' Ebony yelled into the bathroom mirror. She cut her hair so that it almost looked even on the sides, but the back, goodness knows what that looked like. She'd have to wear a hat.

Ebony sat at the kitchen table checking her emails on the laptop while she waited for the colour to set in her hair. Her publisher wanted to speak to her about the book she had recently submitted and asked her to call.

'I won't be,' she said, noticing a message from Outlook saying the sender asked for a delivery and read receipt, and did she want to respond. She clicked "no". Her heart jumped into her throat with fear, but she didn't know why. She turned off the laptop, opening no other emails. She could get them on her phone. At least she still had that connection to her life. How did she still have her phone? Had Café Man forgotten to take it from her?

Ebony's lightning bolt moment, the moment she realised her life, the life she had grown comfortable in, was over, struck as she turned off the computer. She rested her head on her arms on the table and sobbed. The tears were for her friend Gabrielle, warm, caring, special Gabrielle whom she would never speak to again. She cried for James, her ex-boyfriend, and smiled when she thought how much happier they were as friends and not lovers. Tears ran for her parents. Although she wasn't close to them, and only went to Far North Queensland once a year, they were her Mum and Dad. To them all, she was dead.

———

Standing in front of the mirror drying her hair, Ebony decided she was happy with the colour. It suited her, and the wonky haircut didn't look as bad in blonde. She dressed in the new clothes Café Man had picked up for her, put on some lipstick—which she found at the bottom of a drawer in the bathroom—and sun-glasses. She was Felicity Browning, the main character in her latest series: stylish, poised, confident. *If only.*

Pleased to have captured Felicity Browning's look, Ebony sat on the couch waiting for Café Man to text that he was at the door.

'Good morning,' he said, walking into Ebony's living room as if it were his own. 'Why are you dressed like Felicity Browning?'

Ebony's mouth dropped open. Her head moved forward, and her brow furrowed. 'How do you know about Felicity Browning?'

'I've read your books, Ebony. So, why are you dressed like her?'

'I want to get my notebook. It must be at the café.'

'I imagine it is. But you are not going to get it. I will. Tell me about it in case they won't give it to me.'

Ebony explained the small details of her precious notebook to this horrid stranger.

'When I get back, you will be ready to leave. It's time you died and moved on to your new life.'

He left before Ebony could offer any resistance.

The café was busy. Café Man looked around for Tuesday morning's server. He couldn't see her. He waited to be guided to a seat before tackling the person taking his order. 'Hello, a friend of mine was in here last Tuesday. She was shot.' Café Man watched the girl's face blanch. 'Do you know about that?'

'Yes. It was terrible. We are all very upset.'

'As you should be. The young lady was a friend of mine.'

'Was?' the girl asked.

'Oh, yes, you might not know. She died on Friday.'

The girl sat down opposite Café Man. 'From the gunshot?'

'No. Heart failure.'

'Oh, dear. So young. How can I help?'

'She was an author. It appears her notebook was left behind when the ambulance took her away. I can't find it anywhere, and her publisher would like to have it.'

'I'll see if it is in the office.'

A few minutes passed before the young woman reappeared, but to Café Man's angst, no notebook in her possession.

'There is a book. The boss said to ask you what colour it is, and what is written on the first page.'

'It is black, A4 paper size. It has a penholder on the side, but she wrote with a pencil which is probably lost. The first page has a quote from Jim Thompson "There is only one plot — things are not what they seem."

The waitress walked to the back of the café through the doors marked "staff only". Café Man waited. Relief washed over him like the shower he took after he "disposed" of his brother. The girl handed him the notebook.

'Thank you. May I please order a cheese toasty and a flat white with soy milk?' The waitress nodded and toddled off to fill Café Man's order.

4

EBONY

Ebony unlocked the door when Café Man knocked. 'Did you get it? Did you?'

He handed her the notebook. 'Did you pack? Did you?'

Ebony pulled the notebook into her, then held it at arm's length, taking in the comfort it gave her.

'I repeat. Did you pack? A few things. Not much.'

'Not yet,' Ebony confessed. I was too anxious to concentrate. I forgot what you said to do.'

Café Man sighed a sigh of exasperation. 'Put the book down and get a small bag. I'll tell you what NOT to put in it.'

He followed Ebony into the bedroom. 'No toiletries. You died. You can't take toiletries to the afterlife. Undies, pyjamas, a tracksuit, socks. Things that won't be missed. We will buy anything else you need.'

'How will I be able to buy anything? I won't have access to my bank account.'

'Don't worry about that.'

Ebony threw the things she was told to collect into a backpack. 'I'm taking the supplies I bought from the pharmacy.'

'Of course. I'll make sure you don't leave any trace of having been here since your death. Sit down and rest while I go through things.'

———

'Come on. Time to go.'

Ebony's eyes shot open; her heart thumped. 'You frightened me,' she complained. 'Please don't do that again, Café Man.'

'My name is Bradley Hector Culley. You can call me Brad. I prefer that to Café Man. Put on your runners. Detectives Sanderson and Tomy are on their way here. I've done everything to put the apartment back to the just left, not been here for days look.'

'I prefer Café Man,' Ebony sulked. 'And how do you know the detectives are on their way?' Her life was unravelling faster than it did last Tuesday.

'Sanderson is a friend of mine. I'll explain in the car. Get up. We are going.'

Ebony wiped the tears off her face with the back of her hand as she closed the apartment door behind her. The deposit she'd worked hard to save, the mortgage payments she'd made, the furniture she'd bought, all disappeared behind the dark stained timber door.

She did not need as much help going down the back stairs as she had going up them two days ago, but she leaned on Café Man, anyway. He smelled good. A picture of James's chiselled body flashed into her mind. She shook her head. She might use Café Man in one of her stories. Stories she would have to write under another name.

She slid onto the passenger's seat and did up her

seat belt. He put her backpack in the cargo space and got into the vehicle.

'Talk,' Ebony said before he'd even closed the door.

'I cannot give you all the information, Ebony,' he said while checking the reversing camera. 'But as I said to you last week when I shot you, your life is in danger. I was ordered by, well, you don't need to know who, to kill you. It seems you have come across information, whether or not you realise it, that could ruin a great big business. They wanted you disposed of. Out of the way. Out of their hair.'

'How can I be in anyone's hair? That is ridiculous. I don't know what you are talking about. What information? And why didn't you kill me when you were supposed to?'

Brad started the ignition. 'I didn't kill you because I do have some principles. I know you are oblivious to your involvement.'

'Where are we going?' Ebony demanded. 'Have my friends been told I died? What about my parents?'

'The funeral is Thursday this coming week to give your parents time to come down from North Queensland. They'll go through the things in your apartment and start to sort out your affairs.'

Ebony turned to look out the window. She didn't want him to see her crying, but the tears streamed down her cheeks, and her sobbing was relentless. He reached out with his left hand and touched her knee. She pushed him away.

'You said when you resurrected me that there would be a body. Whose body? And how did I die?'

'It doesn't matter who. Sandy sorted that for me. And you died of heart failure.'

'And who is Sandy?'

'Detective Sanderson. He's my best friend.'

'How could someone like you have a best friend?' she yelled.

'That's harsh,' Brad said checking the rear view mirror. 'We are nearly there. Leave any other questions until we get you settled.'

Ebony folded her arms across her chest and stared through the windscreen. It was all too much.

5

———

BRAD

The phone my father contacts me on vibrated in my jacket pocket.

'Hello,' I said when I swiped to answer. One doesn't call my father "Dad" or any other term of endearment. When necessary I call him "Father". He calls me "Junior", not my name. My name is Bradley. Bradley Hector Culley — not Junior. There is no "Jr" after my name. I am the second son, and neither my older brother nor I were named after our father. I answer to whatever he calls me. It makes life easier.

'Come into the office, Junior,' he ordered. 'Now.'

Without answering him, I hung up the phone and did up the seat belt in my black SUV. I like the SUV; it isn't pretentious like the cars my father gets driven around in. It's a hybrid and has all the bells and whistles you'd expect from a vehicle at the top end of the range. I'm not exactly slumming it. But from the outside, it looks like any other SUV.

Pushing the button to have the window go down, I waved my pass in front of the carpark scanner and waited for the barrier to raise. I don't have the luxury of a space with "reserved" on it, but there are plenty of free spaces allocated to the company.

My father's office is on the third floor of this modest building on Exhibition Street, Melbourne. He doesn't believe in spending money on flashy offices when modest will do. Pity he doesn't feel the same way about his cars.

One of his bodyguards, I like to call them "accessories" because they hang off him all the time, waited to escort me to, and up in, the elevator. The mind boggles to think that a twenty-eight-year-old man who was ordered to kill another human being can't make his way up an elevator and into an office. At least the accessory smells nice. I thought about asking him the name of his cologne, but although it wasn't cheap and nasty, probably wasn't on my preferred list of "suppliers".

Father likes his accessories. He likes the burly, brainless guardians who serve him twenty-four-seven. I followed this one like a lost puppy.

'Hello Junior. Sit down.'

I didn't respond to his greeting. He didn't expect me to. I sat obediently and crossed my legs, waiting for the inquisition.

'Is that girl dead? One of my observers thought you missed the mark, and they took her to hospital.'

'She was taken to hospital. I didn't miss the mark. She died a couple of days later, but you would know that. I'm sure you've contacted the coroner. Pity, she was an interesting character.'

Father leaned back in his chair, glaring at me with those piercing grey eyes. The eyes my brother inherited. I have our mother's eyes. Thank God.

He folded his arms over his rotund belly. He'd been in the good paddock for some time.

'Yes, we contacted the coroner. The autopsy said heart failure was the cause of death.'

I smirked to myself. Sandy had done a good job.

'Well done, Junior. Are you going to the funeral?'

I almost choked on fresh air. Well, the air in my father's office wasn't exactly fresh, but there didn't appear to be any nasties floating around in it.

'Why would I go to the funeral?'

'Some assassins like to see their victims laid to rest. Gives them closure.'

I was speechless. How do you react when your father sees you as an assassin? What did he find in me that led him to believe I could kill another human being?

I cleared my throat. 'No, I am not going to the funeral.'

'As you wish. Did you get her notebook?'

My father's question threw me off kilter. How did he know Ebony had a notebook?

'What notebook?' I asked, feigning ignorance.

'She kept a notebook. I want it. I want to know what is in it. Where is it?'

'It must be at the café,' I sputtered, trying to keep my cool. 'I'll spin some sort of yarn that ensures they give it to me.'

Satisfied with my responses, my father dismissed me, and Accessory Two escorted me into the elevator and down to my car.

Seriously?

I called Sandy before I pressed the button to start the ignition. 'I'm leaving my father's office,' I said without waiting for the "hello". 'He appeared placated, believing that our writer is indeed dead.'

'Hello, Brad,' Sandy sniggered. 'Yes, I'm well. Thanks for asking.'

'Don't be cute. I'm trying to keep you in the loop. How are you handling the investigation? Can you trust Tomy?'

'There is no reason not to. She is tenacious but not stupid. When the obvious avenues are exhausted and we do not find a killer, Tomy will move the file into the too hard basket. But it will not go away, Brad. You and I should chat over a drink. I can't talk at work. Meet me tonight at Claude's.'

We hung up simultaneously. I love my friendship with Sandy. I never have to explain myself.

Accessory Two was still standing by the elevator when I finally pushed the ignition button in the SUV. He was obeying his instructions literally, watching until I left the car park. I so wanted to open the window and yell that Elvis was leaving the building, but that would have gone right over his head.

———

Claude's is a bar Sandy and I have frequented since we were at university together. Yes, apart from being a dashing twenty-eight year old, single man, I also have an accounting degree. Sandy has a law degree, but applied to the Victoria Police as soon as he graduated. Wasting time as an article clerk wasn't for him.

Claude's is tucked away in a well-hidden laneway in Melbourne. Well, it was well-hidden until the last couple of years. Now the well-hidden laneways are trendy, and the Gen Z's are squeezing the breath out of priceless little spots like Claude's.

I had trouble finding an empty table with two seats, and when I did, sat facing the door waiting for my friend. I waved the server away with an endearing smile. She would come back when she saw Sandy at the table.

I took my phone out of my pocket and revisited the text messages between Ebony and me. She has no idea what she's done to deserve the wrath of my father. Neither do I. Apparently, she was a threat to the family business. In my father's mind that's the only excuse one needs to take a life.

My brother had been a threat to the family business too.

Sandy sat in the chair opposite. 'Did you order?'

'What?' I asked startled. I hadn't seen him come in, I was so lost in the memories of my older brother and his grey, piercing eyes.

'Did you order?'

'No. I did not. You complain if I order before you get here, you shit.'

'Just checking.'

Sandy —that's what everyone calls him. Most people don't even know his first name is Ryan, took off his jacket, put it on the back of his chair, brushed the shoulders, and sat down as if he were joining the Queen for brunch. Hopeless.

I smiled beatifically at the server, and she sauntered over.

'What can I get you, gentlemen?' she asked.

We each ordered a beer, and I got a plate of loaded fries for us to share.

'So, what's going on?' Sandy was straight to the point.

'Do you have any idea why Miss Makepeace was chosen for elimination?'

He laughed loudly, only stifling the noise when he realised he'd drawn the attention of other patrons.

'Come on, Brad. I don't even talk to your father. How would I know?'

'Just making sure.'

The beers arrived, and I took a gulp of the cold, amber liquid. Sighing with satisfaction as I put the glass on the table. 'I'm going to have to find out. She intrigues me. She's so ordinary. What could she possibly have, on my father or his company? I think the answer is in her notebook. Father asked me if I had it. He wants it.'

'Do you? Have it?'

Sandy's glass was almost empty when the food arrived. He ordered another and asked if I would like one.

No. One is enough for me on a Tuesday night.

'She has the notebook,' I told my friend. 'I got it from the café for her. The ambos left it on the table, and a waitress squirrelled it away in a locker.'

Nodding as if he understood everything, Sandy picked up his fork and attacked the loaded fries. 'I didn't think I was hungry until these hit the table.'

Sandy isn't a crooked cop. On the contrary, he is straight down the line. Except when he's protecting me. They could charge me with murder, but I didn't kill anyone. The body in the morgue is an unidentified young woman with an uncanny resemblance to Ebony. She died of natural causes if you can call a drug overdose, causing heart failure, natural. No identification. She had been on ice for three weeks, with no-one coming forward to claim her. So they will bury her as Ebony Makepeace.

'So, let's recap and make a plan,' I said, hearing my grandmother in my ear: *Don't speak while you have a mouthful.* 'I'll start. From the beginning.

'Number one, Father summons me, saying he has discovered a threat. A threat to the company, to him, and the threat must be vanquished. Yes, he used the word "vanquished". I watched my prey for a couple of weeks, working out her routines, observing her life. I liked her, I liked her weird attire, her aloof presence. I liked how predictable she was. I approached you, Sandy, to see what I could do.

'Number two, you came up with the idea to wound her, not kill her, but she had to be on board.

'Number three, I convinced her, when I sat down at her table, that she was in danger and to follow my lead. She did. She wasn't a fan of being killed and resurrected though,' I said through melted cheese and bacon bits.

'What does Miss Makepeace say about all of this?' Sandy asked as he scoffed the last of the fries.

'Wipe your face. You have sauce all over your chin. She is confused, sad, heart-broken, and incredulous.'

After eating two-thirds of the loaded fries, Sandy leaned back in his chair. He didn't look comfortable, but I let it slide. He sat for a few minutes rocking slightly, eyes darting from left to right, a frown appearing and disappearing, biting his lower lip as his mind ticked over.

I waited.

'First, you have to get the notebook and look through it. Whatever reason your father decided she had to die is in that notebook. He asked you for it, didn't he?'

I nodded. Speaking seemed pointless.

'By the way, the bullet they took out of her in the hospital is missing. Appears the chain of evidence has collapsed.'

'Thank you, Sandy. Are you sure you're okay with this?'

'No, I'm not okay with this. But I had to make a choice to save her life and yours. It seemed a small price to pay for both. I've covered up for now, and as long as your father doesn't get suspicious and start snooping, we'll be good.'

The server came over to the table to see if we wanted anything else. We each ordered a coffee.

6

———

EBONY

Ebony looked through the peephole in the door and groaned when she saw Brad on the other side. He had settled her temporarily in a hotel room in the city overlooking the Melbourne Cricket Ground. It wasn't really a hotel room per se, Ebony had thought when Brad swiped the entry card to let her in. It had a small kitchen, a large bedroom, and a huge open living dining area. The bathroom was luxurious; the spa occupied an area as big as the bathroom and laundry in her own apartment.

Opening the door just wide enough to speak to him without letting him in, she hissed, 'What do you want?'

'You are going to have to let me in. I cannot speak to you through a gap in the door.'

Ebony sighed the sigh of someone exasperated with her situation, but with little recourse to change it. She stepped back, opened the door, and let Brad show himself in. He was, after all, paying for the room.

He sat at the dining table. 'Why don't you make us a coffee, then you can hear me out.' Bradley clasped his hands together on the table, waiting for Ebony to do as he asked.

Ebony put a mug of black coffee in front of Bradley, then set milk and sugar on the table. *He can do that himself.*

'Okay,' Ebony said, sitting down with her hands around her mug. 'Spill it.'

'I've told you my name. You must not repeat it to anyone. Ever. Do you understand?'

Ebony nodded.

Bradley continued. 'They gave me an order to kill you.'

'I know. You told me the day you shot me. And again in the car on the way here.' Ebony grumbled.

'Please don't interrupt. There will be things you know and things you don't. Please listen and take it seriously.'

'I watched you for a couple of weeks to get a feel for your routine, the people you mixed with, so I could work out the best place to do the deed. Over the days, I became quite fond of you and did some research. I discovered you are a talented crime writer and re-alised I had read some of your books. I approached my best friend Detective Sanderson, for help.'

The coffee that had just made it into Ebony's mouth spluttered over the table. Bradley checked to see none of it made its way to his clothing.

'How does a police detective fulfill the role of best friend and conspirator?' Ebony demanded while she wiped the coffee from her face and the table.

'With difficulty. Anyway. Sandy, that's what everyone calls him, came up with the plan. My em-ployer is not like the baddies in your books. He doesn't use high-tech devices like monitoring mobile phones or hacking into people's computers. The task was straightforward — you were a problem — a problem to be dealt with expeditiously.

'Sandy found a body we could use. A poor girl who looked a lot like you. She died from heart failure brought on by a drug overdose, and no one came to claim her. We would pretend you were dead, and she would become you. Then you would leave town, start a new life with a new name, and I would avert a catastrophe.'

Ebony felt sick. Until this point, she could dismiss the whole scenario as fantasy, but her parents burying a girl without a name, thinking it was her, made her stomach churn.

'I still don't get it. Why would anyone want to kill me? I go through life making little ripples on the surface. I don't make waves. Could it be they are mistaken? They have me confused with someone else?'

'Sadly, no. It was clear from the beginning that you were the one.'

'What now?' Ebony huffed. She put her hands on her lap so Bradley wouldn't see them shaking. 'I am so confused, frightened, and alone.'

'You're not alone, Ebony. You don't know me. In fact, I'm the one who put a bullet in your side, so why would you even want to know me. But you can trust me. You must trust me and Sandy. We haven't gone to all this trouble to see you ignore our warnings and advice. We don't want you to meet your demise at the hands of some other thug.'

Ebony stood up and paced the room. 'As I asked before, what now?' She glared at Bradley, waiting for an acceptable response.

'For the immediate future, when you go outside

these walls, wear the disguise you wear so well. Felicity becomes you. When your new documents arrive, we'll plan your future. But before then, I need your notebook.'

Ebony's mouth dropped. 'Why? It's personal. It's the only thing I have left, apart from my phone.'

'I need it. My employer wants it. And I'll take your phone. I'll give you a new one.'

Ebony's stomach lurched and her head spun. She sat down on the couch, leaning forward with her head on her knees.

'Your notebook is the key to this, Ebony. Please get it for me.'

'If you think I'm giving you my notebook, you have another thing coming.' The venom in Ebony's voice sprayed around the room. She had never spoken to anyone like that. Ever.

'Get it for me, please. I'll copy it for you. At least then you will still have something.'

'You need a new employer,' Ebony snarled as she made her way to the bedroom. Pulling the notebook from the drawer in the bedside chest, she pushed it across the kitchen table to Bradley.

Ebony watched as Bradley opened the notebook. She shivered. Her secrets were all in there. The secrets she often put into her stories. He skimmed over the pages without commenting, without looking up, without shifting on his seat.

'Thank you, Ebony,' Bradley said, closing the book. 'I'll copy it for you tomorrow and bring it back. Is that okay?'

'Do I have a choice?'

'No. You see, we have made progress. You do understand the severity of your situation, and although reluctantly, you are cooperating. Thank you. I'll take my leave now. I'll see you tomorrow.'

Ebony closed the door behind him.

'Why does he want *that* notebook? It's the fifth one I've filled up.'

———

Even though he had a swipe card, Brad knocked politely on Ebony's door. She scrambled off the couch, checked the peephole, and opened the door. He handed her the photocopied version of her notebook. Swollen, clunky, ugly.

'Thank you. I think,' she said. 'Are you coming in?'

'Thank you, that would be nice.' Brad closed the door behind him and took up a position on the couch.

'I want to go to my funeral,' Ebony spurted. 'I want to see my parents and my friends for the last time. Can you help me with a disguise?'

'I told my employer I wasn't going to your funeral.'

'So? I wasn't inviting you.'

Brad smirked. 'I deserved that one. Yes, I'll get you a disguise. I'll go now and bring it back soon. Funeral is Thursday.'

'I know when my funeral is,' Ebony snapped. 'And have you thought about the likelihood of my parents wanting to look at my body? A likeness isn't the same as the real thing.'

Brad stared at Ebony. 'Why would anyone want to look at a loved one's body?'

'Seriously? Of course they will. I see them once a year. I died suddenly. They'll want to say goodbye personally.'

'There's the answer to your question then,' Brad

quipped. 'You only see them once a year. If you look a bit different, they can put it down to time. When the funeral is over, we'll work on your permanent re-location.'

Ebony watched him go, glad to see the back of him, yet wishing he'd stayed longer. She realised she was lonely.

She never got lonely.

BRAD

Accessory Two waited for me in the underground car park. He reminded me of an otherworldly creature who spent his life in darkness.

'I'll take the notebook,' he said, stepping forward to prevent me from entering the elevator lobby. 'Mr Culley does not need to see you.'

'Is that right?' I smirked. 'Then in that case, I don't have the notebook.'

Shock swam over Accessory Two's face. He didn't know how to respond to the obstacle I'd thrown in his path.

'You'd better call Mr Culley, because I am not handing over the notebook to anyone but him.'

Accessory Two took his mobile out of his pocket, shook his head when there was no service, and put it back in its place. 'All right then. Follow me.'

'Seriously! I know my way to my father's office, you moron.'

'I don't care. Follow me. Mr Culley doesn't want to see you. You'll have to wait until I've told him what you said.'

'Do you think I'll get sent to the naughty corner or given a detention?'

Accessory Two's eyes glazed over. He didn't know what I was on about.

'I do not need to see you, Junior,' my father roared when Accessory Two let me in.

'Then I don't need to give you the notebook. I want an explanation as to why it is so important.'

'That's none of your concern, Junior.'

The hairs on the back of my neck bristled and my mouth dried up. I so wanted to punch his sanctimonious face.

'Well, it is my concern, Father. You told me to shoot a young woman. A clever young woman in the prime of her life. You told me to do this without explanation. I obeyed you. Then you told me to get her notebook. I've done that. Now, it's my turn. I want to know what you hope to find in the notebook.'

I stood on the other side of my father's ample desk, looking at his ample body. 'I'm waiting,' I challenged.

'For what? I don't know what I'm looking for. I will know when I see it though. I'll be sure to let you know. Have a nice day.'

And with the wave of his hand, he summarily dismissed me. Again. There was no point arguing.

Next time I'm at Ebony's, I'll ask her to show me her copy. I had read through some of the original on another visit, but nothing jumped out at me that would interest my father.

Although my father's office is unpretentious, he is not. He commands attention from anyone in the room with him; he does not suffer fools, and knows he is always right. The company of which he is CEO, belongs to a powerful lobby group that pressures governments to bend to their will. Fossil fuels are his bread and butter, and my brother, who has a master's in environmental science, who travelled to the Southern Ocean one year on a Sea Shepherd expedition, who buys nothing containing palm oil, clashes with our old man. Big time. I should say clashed because my brother disappeared one year ago. Two years after our mother died. Ebony could spin my brother's story into a good yarn.

———

Killing my brother was the first deadly assignment my father gave me. Steven Hector Culley — yes we have the same middle name — our grandfather's, found information about an environmental disaster that had been covered up. Well, at least that's the reason my father gave for the order.

My brother uncovered a few scant notes about acid mine drainage in one of the coal mines in the middle of nowhere, where heavy metals had dissolved and seeped into ground water. Steven challenged our father, threatening to report the company to the Environment Protection Authority and any other organisation that would listen, including the media.

My instructions were clear: get Steven into the car, telling him we were going to look at a new coal mine site. When I had him in the middle of nowhere, I was to shoot him and bury him. Deep.

While we were driving to the pretend site, I told Steven about Father's plan. The poor bloke turned as white as the pages of Ebony's copied notebook. He asked me if I was going to carry out the plan. As clever as my brother is, sometimes he is just plain dumb. I explained that if I was going to carry out Father's plan, why would I tell him. That would make life difficult for me. 'Just as well, your brother is an accountant,' I told him as we pulled up into a neatly presented caravan park in Wonthaggi, a town in Gippsland.

'Why?' Steven asked, still struggling with the concept that his father wanted him dead.

'I've set up bank accounts for you all over the place with new credit cards, new drivers' licence, new passport. In a different name, of course. You will be James Horace Crawford. Do you like that? I think it's romantic.'

'You're a bloody idiot if you think I'm going to run away and call myself James Horace Crawford. Turn the car around, I'm going to the police and the Australian Securities and Investments Commission.'

I pulled the car up next to a palatial on-site caravan and turned off the ignition. 'I've planned everything, Steven. You have three choices: go along with what I've organised and survive and thrive, or go back to Melbourne, tell the authorities, and wait to die, or give in and have me kill you today.'

'He's going to get away with poisoning the water table. What else has he done that we haven't uncovered?'

'Lots of things, I imagine,' I said to my brother as I watched his expression change with his emotions. 'I'll go to the office and get the key for the van. We'll discuss everything once we're inside.' I took the thing-a-me-jig that has to be nearby for the car to start just in case Steven decided he'd scurry back to the city without me.

———

'Pretty flash van,' Steven said, looking from one end to the other.

'Yes, it's twenty-eight feet long. You're going to be here for a few days, so I wanted you to at least have some comfort. A hotel was out of the question. The bed is a queen, there's a full sized toilet and a full sized shower, not one of those cubby holes you see in the vans the grey nomads pull around. Plenty of storage and leather seating around the table.'

Steven's eyes moved from one end of the van to the other. 'Thank you. I think,' he said.

Indicating that my brother should sit at the table, I slid into the other end. 'Let me begin. Please leave your questions until the end of the presentation.' I laughed at my joke.

Steven cracked a tiny smile.

'I packed a few things for you, just the basics, so you've got clean clothes at least. The bag's in the car.'

Steven nodded, and looked at me with those grey, steely eyes. But on him, they didn't pierce my soul like our father's did.

'I've set up bank accounts in your new name, with corresponding EFTPOS cards. There's a passport in your new name, too. I'm glad you never married Joanna because things would be even messier. You're not seeing anyone, are you?' I had not taken my brother's relationship status into account when I decided I wouldn't kill him.

'No. Not seriously. There are a couple of women who might miss me.'

'Good. Then Father will have even more reason to think you are dead.'

'What about my work? I do have a business of my own remember.'

'I guess Father will step in and close it down when your disappearance is confirmed. On that note, I have performed some creative accounting miracles and calculated the worth of your business. Father's coal mining company has bought your environmental flagship business and merged it into his. He just doesn't know it.' I watched Steven process this new information.

'You will have enough money to start again, in another country, both in your business endeavours and your personal life. I've put a lot of planning into this, Steven. You are going to Spain. The Spanish you learned in school will get a workout.'

My brother was completely overwhelmed, and I could relate. It's the feeling of drowning while you're not in the water. I felt it when I realised our father saw me as another accessory, an assassin.

Who asks their accountant son to kill his brother? Someone who sees the dark side of a man. Someone who is evil.

'I'll get us something to eat, and a few groceries to tide you over for the next couple of days. After we've eaten, I'll have to leave. He will work out how long it would take me to drive to the destination, kill you, dig a hole, and bury you.'

Steven shivered. 'Why would he ask you to kill me? Why not employ a professional?'

'Good question, brother. It's something I've struggled with. I pride myself on being nothing like him, but there is a niggle inside my heart that tells me I am fooling myself. He sees a darkness in me.'

'But he can't, not really. You chose not to kill me. Thank you, by the way.'

'I know, but he must see the propensity within me.

I worry that one day he'll ask me to hurt someone I don't care about.'

———

Steven promised me he would stay in the van and the surrounds until he left for Sydney. He would rent a car with his new credit card and drive. I'd allowed three days for the journey, but he would do it in two. A flight to Madrid was booked. He would be okay if he kept his head. I took his phone and gave him a new one. The only number in it was mine.

'I'll call you when I get back to Melbourne,' I said as I closed the van door. 'Keep your cool.'

———

It was hard to stay awake. I'd had a busy few days and not much sleep. The car wandered onto the rumble bars on the side of the road a few times, alerting me to impending danger, and it emanated annoying beeps when it deviated off the straight and narrow to the middle of the highway.

The phone my father called me on danced on the passenger seat as if it were swaying to music only it could hear. I didn't answer it. He kept calling; the phone responded with vibration and disco lights. I found a bay on the side of the road and pulled into it.

'Yes,' I said when my father called me for the fourth time.

'I want photos,' he said.

'What are you talking about?'

'I want photos of your brother's body. A collage of events.'

'Why? Don't you trust me?'

'No,' came the answer I was dreading.

Had he had me followed? *I think not. I was careful.*

'What makes you think I haven't completed the task?' I baited my father, hoping to get a glimpse into what was going on in his head.

'I have my reasons. He is your brother; this is your first job of this nature. Send me the proof.'

'But he is dead and buried, Father. That means I have to return to the scene, remove the dirt, and take the photos you want.'

'Send me the GPS coordinates. One of my men will do it for you.'

Sweat beaded on my forehead. My hands were shaking. *Control yourself.*

'I've not long left the site. I'll go back and do as you ask.'

'Good.' My father hung up.

I called Steven, said I was coming back, would be there in thirty minutes, and I'd explain when I got there.

Before I turned the car around I used Google to find out what makes convincing fake blood. The easiest was ketchup and water. I'd have to stop at the supermarket on the way back. I dismissed using tomato sauce instead of ketchup because I knew it was runnier.

Steven sat at the table at the far end of the van. He was biting his lower lip, tapping his foot on the base of the seat, and turning the phone I gave him over and over in his hands.

'We've got work to do,' I said. 'He wants proof that you're dead. And if I don't send it to him, he's going to get one of his goons to look for your body. If I don't convince him, we're both dead.'

Although Steven was older, he had the look of innocence that is often painted on the face of the youngest in a family.

'What are you going to do?' he said through a voice that hardly broke the surface.

'I got the supplies on the way back. You are going to use ketchup and water to make fake blood. We are going to dig a hole. You are going to lie in said hole with ketchup spread over your shirt, right where your heart is. I will take photos of you in said hole.'

I could see the disbelief, the panic in my brother's eyes. He looked at me, tears streaming down his face.

'Get it together,' I chastised. 'It's all good.'

'I'm in denial, Brad,' he said. 'I can't believe my father would ask my only sibling, the brother I've adored all our lives, to kill me. You are both monsters: him for wanting it done, and you because he assumed you would do it.'

'All of that has gone around and around in my head for days, don't worry about it. But it is what it is, and I can't think of any other way to save us both.'

Steven stood up, took the ketchup off the table, and mixed it in a bowl with some water until he thought he had the consistency of blood. 'Does this look right?' he asked me.

I was about to say how would I know, but that was a superfluous question. He would assume I knew because of what Father had told me to do to him. I nodded.

We put the supplies in the back of the SUV and drove 50km back towards Melbourne. Steven did not speak. I did not engage him. The tension between us was palpable. The landscape differed on either side of the road. On the left was water, and on the right bush. It was the bush we would drive into.

'Have you decided on a location?' Steven startled me when he broke his silence.

'Not really,' I said, turning the car off the road through some scrub. 'It doesn't matter. It's the photos he wants.'

'Then why have we driven all this way if it doesn't matter?'

'I'm pretending it does. I have to be convincing when I talk to him.'

We found a clearing with light weight soil. I turned off the car and got out to collect the shovels from the back. Steven stayed in his seat.

'Are you getting out to help?' I put a shovel over each shoulder.

'I don't trust you. Suddenly I am afraid of my little brother.' More tears streamed down Steven's face, settling in the corners of his mouth.

'I get it,' I said. 'I planned and set up a new life for you. Why would I do that if I was going to put a bullet in your chest? Oh, shit. Shit. Shit.'

'What?'

'He said to shoot you in the back of the head.'

'You're not serious. This gets more horrific by the minute. I need to call triple zero.'

I opened the passenger door and grabbed the phone from Steven's hands. 'Let's just get this part over with so we can both move on.'

Steven stepped onto the ground. He followed me a little further along in the clearing, where I suggested we dig.

It was hard work, even though the soil was reasonably soft underfoot.

We dug a hole about one metre deep. 'It will be dark in an hour,' I said. 'Let's get this over with. Get in.'

Steven's face lost all its colour, his hands shook, and the tears reappeared.

I was losing patience, even though I understood his trepidation. 'We have to make it look real, for God's sake. Otherwise he'll kill both of us. Where's the ketchup?'

'On the floor of the backseat,' Steven's voice quivered while he struggled to keep his composure.

I retrieved the ketchup and told him again to get in the hole. This time, he obeyed.

'Lie down with your head tilted to one side a little.'

I climbed into the hole, straddling Steven's body, and dripped ketchup on his shirt while his heart thumped underneath. I didn't have any experience of what a gunshot wound should look like, but had searched online earlier and followed the pattern of a bullet wound at close range. Steven looked a mess. I took out my phone and told him to leave his hands by his sides and close his eyes. I climbed out of the hole and shovelled dirt over his body, trying to make it look as if he had been covered up earlier.

'Hold your breath. I'll throw some dirt on your face and around your head.' I took more photos than I would need, but I had to be prepared.

'Wipe the dirt from around your eyes and nose.'

I pulled an unused tissue out of my pocket and lent down on the edge of the grave and passed it to my brother. 'Put this over your face. I'll cover your face last. 'I have to throw dirt on you and take more photos.'

Steven's eyes popped open, and the terror within pierced my heart. I watched him put the tissue over his nose and eyes. He took a deep breath. I shovelled dirt on his face and chest, covering him up. Dropping the shovel, I took four photos.

'Get up,' I called to my brother. I helped him out of the hole, and we looked at the photos together.

'Are they convincing do you think?' he asked me.

'I hope so. That's why I told you not to breathe. He will zoom in on every bit of these photos to be sure. I even took one that shows a bit of ketchup. See? I've done what he ordered. They look good to me. Let's fill in the hole and get out of here.'

Steven, dirt stuck to the ketchup on his shirt, in his hair and around his eyes, pulled me in and gave me a hug.'

8

EBONY

Felicity Browning's shoes crippled Ebony, but she struggled through. She wouldn't wear anything so impractical, but Felicity did, and if she wanted to attend her own funeral, she had to look like someone else.

The taxi pulled up to the curb a couple of hundred metres from the entrance to the funeral parlour. She'd planned her arrival to be five minutes after the scheduled starting time, so she could slip in unnoticed, but mourners were still milling outside. The service had not started on time.

'Keep the meter running,' Ebony said to the driver. 'I'm not getting out just yet.'

Fifteen minutes passed with the meter ticking over dollars as if they were pieces of confetti at a wedding. When the last mourner moved into the little chapel, Ebony handed the driver two fifty-dollar notes and told her to keep the change. It was Brad's money; she didn't care how much the fare cost.

Balancing on the heels she'd squeezed her feet into, Ebony pushed open the chapel door and slunk into a seat at the back. A few people turned to look at her. On one side of the chapel were the backs of heads she recognised: her parents, her friend Gabrielle, her ex James's current girlfriend, and the waitress from the café. On the other side in the second row were two men she did not recognise, and about twenty men and women, all sitting quietly, respectfully, from the third row down.

James was at the pulpit wiping tears as he spoke of Ebony's gracious spirit, her giving nature, the way she cared about others more than herself, and above all, what a wonderful writer she was. The two men Ebony did not know nodded in unison when James mentioned her writing, and the young people clapped. A spontaneous recognition of Ebony's life's work. She stifled tears. She had no idea anyone other than her parents and friends would bother to turn up to her funeral.

The service concluded with her parents touching the coffin, saying their last goodbye, and moving towards the door. Ebony slid down the end of the row to the last seat, away from the entrance, and watched everyone leave. Her parents stood at the door shaking hands with the other mourners, thanking them for coming. Her ears pricked when she heard one of the unknown men introduce himself to her parents.

'I am Douglas Culley,' the taller of the two said, shaking her father's hand. 'I am Ebony's publisher. Or to be more precise, I own the company that published Ebony's books.'

'Thank you for coming,' Ebony's mother whispered.

'Our lawyers will be in touch about future royalties, Mrs Makepeace, and to chat about you providing us with the notebook Ebony used for her story planning. Our sincerest condolences.'

'Certainly. I will see if we can locate the notebooks. She used one for each story.'

Ebony searched anxiously for another exit. There was one at the front of the chapel. She headed to it before someone asked her how she knew Ebony Makepeace, or even worse, if one of her fans recognised Felicity Browning. Heart pounding, hands sweaty, knees shaking, head thumping, she stepped into the laneway at the back of the chapel.

'Douglas Culley, Douglas Culley, Douglas Culley,' she repeated the name under her breath. How could he be her publisher? *He must be Brad's father*. It is not a common name, couldn't be a coincidence. But her publisher was a woman. The emails came from Sophie Marris. Ebony shook her head, realising how naïve she had been. Just because someone used a female name on email, didn't mean they were. But Sophie had been friendly, supportive.

I am an idiot.

9

BRAD

I put Ebony's new identity papers, credit cards, and some cash in a leather document holder and zipped it closed. I threw it on the passenger seat and drove towards the hotel.

Today I would resettle her permanently. Her funeral was over, Father seemed placated, and Sandy had slowed down the "murder" investigation. I hadn't spoken to her since yesterday's funeral, and was looking forward to her recount of the event.

Tapping quietly on the door, I waited for Ebony to let me in. Instead of the subdued greeting I usually received, she flung open the door and took up the space, hands on hips, feet apart, with a scowl that would freeze Christmas.

'Oh, hello Ebony. You startled me.'

'Really? I startled *you*. That's rich.'

'May I come in so the whole hotel isn't privy to our conversation?'

She stepped aside. 'We are not having a conversation. We are not friends; this is not amicable. I will ask questions, and you will answer.'

Clearly something had upset the apple cart since I saw her last. I sat on the couch and waited.

'What is your father's name?' she demanded. Her fists were clenched, and her jaw tightened when she finished speaking. Serious stuff. I was sure I could smell the rage, sulphur-like, as if from a volcano.

'Why?'

'Because I asked you, that's why.'

I didn't see any point in keeping Father's name from her. She knew my name so could probably find Father's easily online. 'His name is Douglas Culley. He's an arsehole.'

Ebony paced the room. She stomped up and down without speaking, without looking at me. I waited.

'What's going on?' I asked after about five minutes of her pacing and glaring.

She sat down on the opposite couch, leaned forward, and sneered. 'He was at my funeral.'

'What?'

'HE WAS AT MY FUNERAL,' she yelled. 'He told my mother he was my publisher.'

Now it was my turn to get up and pace. I always found it easier to think while moving, but this time, my mind was blank and stayed that way. I sat down again.

'I don't get it. Why would he say he was your publisher?'

'Because he is. I looked it up. He owns the company that publishes my books. One would think he would be like an absent parent, letting others run things, but apparently not. He is a wonderful, hands on boss who takes a special interest in his publishing house and the books they produce.'

I was speechless. Well, almost. 'There must be a

connection between you as one of his authors, and him wanting you dead. Shit.'

'I knew it,' Ebony roared. 'He is your "employer". How could you not have worked this out?'

'I didn't know he had a publishing company. Honestly, I didn't.' As the words came out, I realised how pathetic they sounded. 'I only know of his mining business.'

As I watched Ebony process the information, I wondered how many other pies my father had his fingers in. How many other people had he disposed of when they got in his way or rained on his parade?

'Get out. I need time to think, to process.' Ebony pointed at the door.

'I'm not going anywhere. We will work through this together, and you are leaving this hotel today. You have to start a new life.'

We stood at the same time, face to face between the two couches.

'I can't take any more of this, Brad,' she whispered. 'My parents were devastated at my funeral. Gabrielle and James were distraught. It broke my heart.'

I put my arms around her and pulled her toward me. She rested her head on my shoulder. She didn't flinch when I stroked the back of her neck. She didn't pull away when I told her I would help her work it out. But I felt my willy swelling, throbbing. I was not up for Ebony to feel it through her leggings and reject me, so I said I would put the kettle on. She plonked back down on the couch, pushed her hair back, folded her arms across her chest, and watched me.

I opened the fridge to get the milk out and noticed two vanilla slices — big ones — yummy looking in a container. 'Who are the vanilla slices for?' I asked over the fridge door.

'Us. I bought them on Wednesday. If I'd known about your father then, I would have only bought one. You would have missed out.'

Did I detect a tinge of humour in her voice, or was that wishful thinking? Did she believe me about my lack of knowledge of my father's business ventures?

'May we have them now?' I asked, taking the milk out.

'I guess so. I'm leaving, so they'll only end up in the bin.'

I put two mugs of tea on a tray, with two small plates, each of which had a spoon and a vanilla slice sitting proudly.

Vanilla slices are my favourite dessert.

'Here you go,' I said as I pulled the coffee table between us and put the tray on it. 'Thank you for the vanilla slice. They are my favourite.'

'I hope you choke on it,' she said.

Is that a twinkle in her eye, or had she been crying?

'Oh, I hope not. I'll be careful.' I watched her as she watched me. 'Are you going to eat yours?'

'When I'm ready. No. You can't have it.'

I wasn't wrong. I had felt the ice breaking between us. She believed me. What a relief. I scoffed my vanilla slice and washed it down with the tea. 'That was delicious.'

Ebony pulled the top pastry sheet that held the icing off her vanilla slice, picked up the spoon and used it to eat half the custard. Then she put the icing sheet on the remaining custard and took a bite.

'That's a great way to eat it,' I said in awe. 'I

wouldn't have thought of that. I just take a bite and deal with the fallout.'

'I noticed,' she said, wiping her mouth with a serviette. 'What are we going to do about your father?'

There was nothing to be done. Pieces of the puzzle were falling into place, but there were still just as many missing. He owned the company that published her books, but that didn't go anywhere near explaining why he ordered her assassination.

'I don't see him unless I am summoned,' I told Ebony. It was the truth. 'There isn't a gap between you and I knowing he is your publisher and him ordering me to kill you — there is a chasm.'

'Well, that unknown will have to become a known. I can't go on without finding the truth. I hate you, you know.'

'Your standards are slipping, Ebony. You used "unknown" followed by "known", then "know", in those three sentences.' I waited for her to slap me.

'I have to finish throwing my few belongings into the backpack,' she said, walking to the bedroom.

I cleaned up the mugs and plates and put them in the cupboard. The hotel room had come fully furnished with crockery, cutlery, and linen. Nothing to put in boxes.

10

EBONY

'Where are you taking me?' Ebony growled as Brad opened the passenger door for her.

'I'd like it to be a surprise. Can you wait?'

'No.' Ebony stared at him, her patience running out. 'It's been a very difficult twenty-four hours. No, it's been a very difficult two weeks. No more surprises, no more secrets.'

'Okay, fair enough,' he said, looking sideways at her.

'I bought a house on a large block in Daylesford. It's walking distance to the town.'

'So you're going to park me in the middle of nowhere? It's bad enough that I have no friends, no family, now I'll have no one around me either. Great.' Ebony sulked.

'Woo, I didn't expect that amount of vitriol. That certainly got a rise out of you. Do you want the truth now?'

'It's not funny, Brad. I'm feeling fragile, please don't play with my psyche.'

'I'm sorry. I own a house on the Altona foreshore.

The tenants' lease expired, and I told the agent not to renew it.

Ebony sat up straight in her seat. She loved the beach—the smell of the salt, the sand underfoot, the feel of the wind. Once a year she took a cottage on Phillip Island and used the time to relax and revive.

'Are you playing with me again?'

'No.'

The journey took on a more interesting vibe, and Ebony became more excited as the kilometres of the Western Freeway slipped by.

———

Brad used the remote to open the garage and went to open Ebony's door, but she was already out of the car. He grabbed her backpack from the back seat and watched her face as it went from surprise to awe in the space of a few seconds.

'Do you like what you see?'

'So far,' she answered. 'Let's go in.'

He motioned to the inside door that led to the house.

The door opened into a hallway. Ebony did not know which direction to look in first.

'Let's start at the front,' Brad said, putting his hand in the middle of her back and guiding her to the front door.

'We share this wall with the house next door,' he said, touching the plaster as if Ebony needed to be shown which wall he was talking about. 'There are two bedrooms and a bathroom downstairs.' He waved his hands as they walked past said rooms. 'And the tour down here finishes with this lovely open plan living, dining, kitchen space, which expands via French doors to the outdoor entertaining area.'

'You sound like a real estate agent,' Ebony said as she moved through the living space touching the surface of the island bench, opening the doors of the wall oven and the dishwasher, and running her fingertips along the dining table surface.

'Let me show you upstairs.'

She followed him.

At the top of the staircase, Brad showed her another living room with a window that took in a vast expanse of Port Phillip Bay, filtered by the Norfolk Island pines that lined the foreshore. The master bedroom with ensuite sat at the rear of the second level, overlooking the garden and the rooftops of neighbouring houses.

'It's magnificent,' Ebony cooed. 'I couldn't afford anything like this. How long will I stay here?'

Brad held out his hand to her. She placed hers in his. 'Let's go downstairs and I'll explain your new life.'

Ebony made herself comfortable on the couch while Brad busied himself in the kitchen.

'Where did all the supplies come from?' she asked.

'I hired a firm to clean — not that it was dirty — and to fill the pantry and fridge. An interior designer did the furniture and the kitchen equipment, like crockery, cutlery, glasses, small electrical. I have to admit I don't know if you cook.'

Ebony watched him and wanted to throw fistfuls of questions at him, but she decided to wait until he had finished making coffee and sandwiches.

He placed their lunch on the dining table and beckoned Ebony to join him there.

'Thanks,' she said, picking up a coffee mug. 'Now, tell me what's going on. And where is my laptop?'

Brad waited until he'd finished half a sandwich before speaking. 'Your new life. You can't be Felicity Browning, so I've created a new you—you are Sherryn Forbes. I left your laptop in your apartment.' He watched her process the information.

'Keep going. I'm listening.'

'Sherryn Forbes can be anyone she wants to be, even a writer. I assume that everything on your laptop was backed up to your OneDrive or Google Drive?'

Ebony nodded.

'You have a Medicare card, a driver's licence, a birth certificate.'

Ebony interrupted him. 'I can sort of imagine how you got new plastic cards, but a birth certificate? How is that possible?'

'Anything is possible if you have the right connections and enough money.'

'Go on.'

'Credit cards, EFTPOS card, and bank accounts set up in the UK.'

Ebony swallowed the last of her coffee. 'Where did the money come from? Who do I have to repay for all of this? And this house, what's the story there?'

'I am an accountant, Ebony. One day, the arsehole will work out what I've done with the funds from one of his companies, but I will be long gone by then. He took everything away from you. I got some of it back. Your parents will get the proceeds from the sale of your apartment, you have nothing.'

Brad handed a manilla folder to Ebony and told her to open it. Wondering what other surprises he had in store for her, she turned the corner of the front cover revealing a wad of documents. She looked at him. The first document was a list of logins and passwords: a new email account, a new internet account, credit card log in, and bank account log in. Bank statements showing a balance Ebony could only have ever dreamed about, followed.

'That's a lot of money,' she said. 'Royalties and the sale of my North Melbourne apartment would never have yielded me two million dollars.'

'Yes they would. Ebony Makepeace could have written books for another forty years. And your apartment would have kept increasing in value.'

Brad smiled; a smile Ebony had not noticed before. He had light brown hair, and his face was almost the same colour, but when he smiled, his white teeth sparkled and lit up his face, spreading to his sky-blue eyes.

'What?'

Ebony shifted in her seat. 'Nothing. How long will it be before your father misses the money and I have to run again?'

'A long time. And you won't have to run again. There is no way he will track the missing funds to you. Me, he might, but he will have to find me.'

Brad reached across the table, and Ebony took his hand. 'Will we christen the bed?' he asked, face as red as the kettle and matching toaster sitting on the bench. She nodded.

Still holding her hand, Brad led Ebony upstairs. He sat on the end of the bed, patting the spot next to him. She sat and turned to look into those eyes.

'Your eyes are a very distinctive blue.'

'My mother's eyes. My brother has our father's eyes.'

'Tell me about your brother,' Ebony encouraged.

'Not today. Today we have more important things to do.' He lay back on the bed and pulled her onto him. Ebony giggled while he tried to undo the zip on her jeans.

'I've never heard you laugh,' he said before kissing her.

Pushing herself off him, Ebony stood and started to remove her clothes. 'You too,' she smiled. 'It will be easier.'

They lay in each other's arms on the new bed, with new linen, in the new house, each staring at a face they had not before taken the time to study.

'Are you staying here?'

'I'll stay the rest of the day and tonight, but I'll have to go tomorrow. I'll be back again soon, though, he said, kissing her, fondling her breasts, moving his hand down her belly and between her legs.

———

While Brad was in the shower, Ebony put four slices of bread in the toaster and put the kettle on. She liked the red. The bench top and splash back were a crisp white, and the red stood out. He came down the stairs while she was buttering the toast.

'Thanks,' he said, skipping the last three steps. 'I don't eat breakfast.'

'Hmm, another thing I don't know about you,' Ebony said, putting her two pieces on a plate.

'I'll be going. I'll call you later today.' He moved to

her side of the bench and leaned in to kiss her. 'I don't want to be away from you too long.'

She watched him walk up the hallway and close the garage door behind him. Even though she'd enjoyed the company of the night before, she was glad to have some space. It was time to think about where her life was going.

11

BRAD

It's a nuisance having two phones, but it's the only way I can keep my father's interference in my life under control. When I go to his office, one of the accessories always takes my phone. In my mind's eye, I can see him sitting in a little dark room surrounded by monitors, looking through my mobile to see who I've been communicating with.

Said phone, often finding itself thrown into the glove box or onto the passenger seat, started dancing around on the seat next to me. I don't connect it to the Bluetooth in the car. Hearing my father's acerbic voice in stereo is not ideal. I am, however, a responsible driver, so I pulled into a parking space on the side of the road and turned off the ignition. Theoretically, if you are behind the wheel with the motor running and on the phone, you are breaking the law. And I am a law-abiding citizen.

I hadn't answered it in the thirty seconds the telephone company allocates to my incoming calls, so waited until my father called again. He always did.

'Yes,' I said after swiping my finger up the screen to answer.

'Where are you? You didn't go home last night.'

My stomach lurched up into my throat and I had to swallow the bile down quickly before I vomited. 'What are you talking about?' I spat.

'Just as I said, Junior. You have not been home. What have you been up to?'

'I have a business, you know. And I have a new lady friend. She's been keeping me busy, not that that is any of your business.' I looked towards the heavens to a god I didn't believe in, praying that my bravado would be convincing.

'*Tsk*,' came from the other end of the call. 'Come into the office.'

'Why? I'm busy. I have a client to see.'

'Care factor?' My father hissed before hanging up.

———

A different accessory waited for me in the elevator foyer. I wanted to mock him and ask if he was a "temp" filling in until the others reappeared. But I wasn't in the mood. My day had started blissfully. Now I was going to see *him*.

'Sit down, Junior,' he ordered when the accessory pointed in the direction of the seat on the other side of my father's desk. The theatrics were mind-numbing.

'I'll stand. I won't be here long.'

'Sit down, Junior. You have no way of knowing how long you will be here.'

He had a point. If I knew what he wanted, I might have gauged the time I would waste in this suffocating office. But I didn't know. I sat down and folded my arms over my chest.

'So we are in a defensive stance as usual I see,' my father scoffed.

'What do you want, Father? I put my client off for an hour.'

'I want ALL of Ebony Makepeace's notebooks and I want her laptop.'

He leaned back on his expensive, black leather, rocking, swivel chair, rested his arms and interlaced his fingers, putting his index fingers into a triangle and touching his mouth with them. Combined with the scowl and those horrid grey eyes, it was enough to give a child nightmares.

'I'm waiting,' he said.

'What other notebooks? You told me to get her notebook. I went to the café and got it. I don't know about any other notebooks.' I waited for the retort; it came quickly enough.

'Well, her mother told me she had a collection of notebooks. There was usually one for each story, but sometimes two stories would go into one notebook. Where are they?'

This called for quick thinking. 'When did you speak to her mother?' I asked as innocently as I could. 'And why would you need to?'

It was my father's turn to squirm in his seat. The usually meticulously planned interrogation of his youngest son had stumbled.

'Why and when I spoke to her mother is not important. It's none of your concern. Where are the notebooks?'

'I don't know,' I said convincingly because I really didn't know. 'Maybe one of her friends has them.'

'Possibly,' he said, tapping his index fingers together. 'And the laptop?'

'Are you serious?' I huffed. 'You told me to kill her, not take an inventory of her life, her belongings.'

'Where were you last night?'

In my early teens, I learnt how to keep myself from blushing with fear or embarrassment. I drew on those skills before I spoke. If I flushed, he would know I was hiding something.

'I am a twenty-eight-year-old man, whom you think is old enough and reliable enough to kill his own brother, without reason, and to murder a total stranger who minded her own business all the time. You will not keep tabs on me in my private life. I will stay where I choose when I am not directly in your employ.' I stood up.

He didn't respond. I wasn't sure if he was speechless, or thought my answer was reasonable and didn't require clarification. Either way, I turned and left. He didn't stop me.

———

While heading to the meeting with my client, I called Ebony.

'Hi there,' I said cheerfully. 'Miss me?'

'What is it, Brad?'

After the night we had, I was a bit miffed by her greeting; it was aloof.

'I've just finished a meeting with my father. There is another complication. When I've finished my client meeting, I'll head back to Altona.'

'Can't you tell me over the phone?'

I was hurt and even more determined to see her. Something was wrong. 'No. I will see you around five.' I hung up.

I struggled to stay focused for my client. Scraps of my father's uncharacteristic faux pas wandered through my mind followed by the replay of Ebony's cool response. My client did not notice my vagueness and as she was leaving my office, thanked me for my excellent attention to detail. That was a relief. Seems I was becoming more proficient at hoodwinking people. I hoped my father was still counted in that number.

After some more housekeeping at the office, I told my assistant, Ferdinand, that I was leaving; he could cope with anything that popped up. Unlike my father's place of business, my office was opulent, in one of the best buildings in the city, with commanding views over the Yarra River and towards the Shrine of Remembrance. I attracted wealthy clients; I had to look the part.

I didn't go straight to Ebony's; I went home first. My father threw me when he wanted to know why I wasn't at home the night before. As my car approached the sensor, the garage door opened, and I drove into the space that was just big enough for my SUV. A small remote buried in my jacket pocket both turned off the alarm and unlocked the door between the garage and the house. Heaven forbid I should ever lose it. I'd long ago forgotten the backup code.

Although the house was as I left it two days ago, I felt an unease as I walked into the bedroom—a feeling of being watched. I shook my head. That was not possible. Everything was just as I left it.

That's something else Ebony does not know about me. I cannot stand mess. I cannot bear it when items are not in their allocated space. You can pick up something to use it, I will let you do that, but you must put it back where you found it when you've finished with it. And if required, clean it first.

Yes, I know, it's called OCD, but I don't find it a trial. It's part of me, who I am. My mother had it too. My brother missed that gene.

The feeling of unease followed me into the kitchen. I opened the fridge, took out the milk, and smelled it. All good. I made a quick cup of tea.

My imagination is awesome. As a kid I had a pretend Burmese Mountain Dog as a pet; she lived a long, long, time. Longer than a real one would. I had three pretend cats who weren't allowed out of my room and pretend friends who liked me. My mother knew about my pretend world, and she would sit with me on my bed and ask me questions about how my pets and friends were going, and what we had been up to. I miss her.

Back to my imagination. I tried to convince myself no-one was watching. The house was as secure as Fort Knox. I am the only one who can get in. As those words rolled around in my head laughing themselves into a stupor, I knew I was being an idiot.

Until the being-watched-feeling proved to be a non-event, I called Ebony from outside. I opened the front door and stepped onto the front porch of my beautifully renovated South Melbourne terrace. But this was not far enough away, so I went for a stroll up the street. I needn't have bothered; Ebony did not answer.

'She is probably in the shower, or walking along the beach.' I disconnected.

Leaving a message was pointless. Her phone would show that she missed my call, so I sent a text message telling her not to call me back, that I would reach out again soon. Love that lingo "reach out again." *Why did I write that?* Checking the phone was on silent, I put it in my pocket and went back inside.

No sooner I'd stepped into the hallway than the tell-tale vibration of an incoming call danced in my pants pocket. It would be Ebony. I told her not to call me back. *Is something wrong?*

As nonchalantly as possible, I moved to the bedroom and prepared for a shower that I would not take. I closed the bathroom door and turned on the tap, before pressing the redial button on the mobile. This time, she answered.

'I just saw your text. Sorry. I'll hang up.'

'No, that's fine. I want to fill you in. When I left your place this morning, my father called me to his office, and among other things, wanted to know where I was last night.'

'Before you go on,' she interrupted. 'It sounds like you're in the shower, can you do something about that?'

'No. I am in the bathroom with the shower running. May I finish?'

No response.

'I think I'm being watched. I don't know how, or if I am being paranoid, but I think my house is bugged. Not taking any chances. I'll drive to the shops to see if I'm being followed, and let you know.'

'Brad. I'm frightened.'

'Don't be. I'll take care of it.'

12

EBONY

'If Brad is being watched, I'm done for.' Ebony paced up and down in the kitchen of her new home. 'No. I'm not. I have a whole new identity. A new life.'

She grabbed the house keys from the hook on the inside of the door on the walk-in pantry, put on her jacket, and slung her shoulder wallet over her head.

Ebony stood at the front gate of her two-storey, modern home taking in the vista of Port Phillip Bay that stretched out before her. She turned to look at the house—a good look—and wondered what old property they had pulled down to make way for this ultra-modern construction. She loved the convenience of the contemporary interior, but was saddened when she looked around at the other houses on the street — some old and in various stages of disrepair. She imagined their owners holding out to the highest bidder. Some like hers were ultra-modern and not likely to stand the test of time like their predecessors did so gallantly.

Ebony hadn't been to Altona for about four years, but apart from the new homes devouring the older ones, it hadn't really changed. She checked the location on her phone to see how long it would take to walk to the main shopping centre in Pier Street – from memory, that's where the cafés were. She would try a few before nominating one as her favourite.

The walk would take sixteen minutes, and it was 1.3 kilometres.

'This is a very civilised location,' she said, putting her phone in her bag and heading to the shopping strip. She wiped tears as the thought of sharing the location with Gabrielle and James popped into her head. Her two friends were in North Melbourne, where her one-bedroom, one bathroom, tiny kitchen and living room apartment, was being sold by her parents. She paid $290,000 for it five years ago. Another one in the block sold for half a million a few weeks before Brad blew a hole in her side and ruined her life.

The just over one kilometre walk took longer than sixteen minutes. Ebony had dawdled, taking in the neighbourhood, and trying to come to terms with the turmoil that had become her life. She wanted to talk to Gabrielle, to tell her she'd slept with Brad, she wanted her friend to tell her everything would be all right.

Ebony expected the street to be reasonably quiet. It was Wednesday. She knew it got madly busy at the weekends and during the summer holidays, but this was neither. She wondered how many people were locals and why there were so many people who didn't seem to work. There were several nicely presented cafés along the street and an ice-cream shop which she promised herself to try one day. *Not today*. Today was a cheese toasty and flat white run through.

She walked past the first two with a mental note to try them another day. One further up the street seemed more her style, so she went inside. It wasn't clear to Ebony what she was supposed to do, wait to be seated or seat herself. Was there table service, or did she order at the counter like in a pub? She stood. The café wasn't busy. She waited. After a few minutes of looking around for someone to notice her, Ebony turned and left. She walked back to one of the cafés she had earlier dismissed.

The greeting was warm, the smile welcoming. 'Table for one?'

'Yes, thank you,' Ebony replied.

'By the window, or at the back? Do you have a preference?'

Ebony reminded herself that looks can deceive. She had dismissed this little café when she walked past it. 'I would like to sit by the window, please. It's a lovely day.'

'Certainly.' The young woman with a Scandinavian accent showed Ebony to a table. 'Are you having lunch?'

'Yes, thank you.' Ebony wanted to ask the woman where she was from, but thought it might be forward. If she came here regularly, she would ask.

The young woman handed Ebony a standard menu and a specials one. 'The bruschetta is wonderful,' she said, pouring water into a glass. 'Can I get you a coffee to start?'

'I would like a soy milk latte, please,' Ebony answered. 'Hot.'

The woman nodded and left her to read the menus.

Ebony had decided to try the bruschetta even though the image of a well-made cheese toasty spun around in her head. While she waited for the coffee to arrive, she looked around the space. A story was already forming in her head, but she didn't have a notebook or a laptop to expand the ideas that sprouted like weeds.

The story would include the Scandinavian woman and this café, which tried to be understated in a pretentious way. If that were possible. The floors were polished concrete and showed signs of wear in the heavy traffic areas. The tables and chairs were mismatched, and either came from op-shops or were expensive try-hards. One wall had pictures of customers, but Ebony was thrilled to see they weren't famous people, just ordinary folk enjoying each other's company and, she hoped, the food. They'd painted the remaining walls in a musk pink that gave the impression the room glowed.

If the coffee and food are up to standard, I might not have to look any further.

Ebony burned her tongue on the coffee. She smiled. It was hot. The bruschetta smelled like garlic and tomatoes soaked in oil, and had to be eaten with a knife and fork. The slice of sourdough bread took up the whole plate, and Ebony thought she could eat that on its own. An image of a cheese toasty made with this bread pushed its way into her head. The server was correct; the bruschetta was the best she had tasted. The slices of avocado gave the dish a creamy balance. *Oh my God, I sound like a TV cooking judge.* She used the napkin to cover her giggle.

After finishing her lunch, she ordered another coffee and leaned back in the chair, watching people meandering up and down the street. Some people were in a desperate hurry and weaved in and out between other pedestrians, while others strolled along without a care in the world. Every second person had a dog on the end of a lead. While Ebony was thinking about whether she should get a small dog, the phone beeped that she'd missed a call. She didn't hear it ring. It could only be Brad; he was the only one with the number.

She took the phone out of her wallet and checked – it was Brad. She decided not to call him back straight away. If it were important, he would call again.

Ebony paid for her lunch, thanked the young woman for the service, and set off in the opposite direction from the one she walked in to get to Pier Street. This time she was going to walk along the beachfront. Further, but on a day like today, more pleasant.

She walked along the beachfront before finding an empty bench seat. A southerly was blowing, and it picked up the smells of the seaweed as it threw itself in Ebony's face. The waves lapped angrily on the shore, as if annoyed that the wind was telling them which way to go. No one was in the water, something she knew would be very different in the warmer weather. Although there could be some very warm days in spring, this was not one of them. While she had space around her, and was free from the head clutter of Brad and his warnings and fear, she took stock of her situation.

Did she really want this life? Until she developed new relationships, it would be very lonely. The thought of Brad as her only friend made her shiver. Until she saw and heard Brad's father talking to her mother at her funeral, she had doubted Brad's story, thought it a fanciful fabrication. Something that only occurred in stories and movies.

A gust of wind picked up sand and blew it at Ebony's legs, and a small flock of seagulls strolled around not too far from her, sizing up the food situation. Each time she took a hand from her pocket to wipe her nose or push her hair out of her eyes, a couple of seagulls would hurry on the sand to see what she was doing.

As the wind moved to a south-westerly, Ebony pulled her jacket around her and headed off toward "home". It was while the thought of heading "home" played in the cobwebs that had developed in her head that she decided she would not be staying.

13

SANDERSON (SANDY)

Detective Sanderson listened as his partner, Tomy, rattled off a list of possibilities in the Ebony Makepeace murder case. Her black shoes were highly polished as usual, her crisp, tailored dark grey suit hugged her body as if she were born in it, and there was not a hair out of place. She looked like this every day, and Sandy often wondered how much time she spent getting ready for work each morning.

'What are you looking at?' she snapped when she noticed his stare.

'You. How long does it take you to get ready for work?'

'What? Since when have you been interested in how I look? Just focus.'

Her latest theory was that Miss Makepeace was mistaken for someone else, and paid the price for being boring. She grumbled about the missing bullet.

'It will eventually go in the Cold Case file, Tomy. Perhaps one day the bullet will surface, and the investigation can continue.' Sandy watched his partner mull over his words, and then summarily dismiss them.

'I am not going to put this in the Cold Case file, the too hard basket. That's not happening. Let's go to her apartment before her parents sell it. Another snoop around. We might have missed something.'

'The search warrant has expired,' he reminded her.

'We are not searching; we are looking around to see if we missed anything.' She smirked at Sandy. 'See, I can manipulate words to suit the situation too.'

Sandy took his jacket off the back of his chair and waited while Tomy got her things together. 'I'll meet you in the garage,' he said. 'You get the car. You can drive. I'm going to the bathroom.'

As they walked in opposite directions, Sandy got his phone out, ready to call Brad. The bathroom was empty. He sat in a cubicle on a toilet. 'Don't interrupt. Listen,' he said when Brad answered. 'Tomy is on the warpath again. We're going to Ebony's apartment to snoop around. Is there anything you want me to look for?'

'Grab her laptop if it's there. Can't have my dear father getting his hands on that. There are supposed to be more notebooks too. See if you can find them. I want them before Father manipulates Ebony's mother into handing them over.'

'This is a new development,' Sandy said. 'Why does he want more notebooks and how did he know about them?' The bathroom door opened and footsteps clomped on the tiled floor. 'Gotta go.' Sandy hung up. He flushed the toilet, washed his hands, and went to the garage.

'Geez, you took long enough,' Tomy scolded. 'Blokes shouldn't take that long.'

'Don't be sexist. I'm here now. Just drive.'

———

'Where did you get the key?' Sandy asked Tomy as she unlocked the door to Ebony's apartment.

'What? Where have you been? Don't you remember? Her mother told the estate agent to give us one whenever we wanted it. I told the agent yesterday that I'd need it.' She grinned.

Sandy shook his head. He didn't remember this conversation with Ebony's mother.

'How did you think we were going to get in?' Tomy asked as she opened the door and stepped inside.

'I assumed we would meet the agent here.'

'You know what happens when we *assume*,' she said mockingly, pushing her hair behind her ear. 'I don't want to be an ass.'

'It's small, isn't it?' he asked as they stepped inside.

'Yes, but it's in a fantastic location. It has everything you would want. Did I tell you I'm thinking of buying it?'

'No. Really? I had no idea you were looking to move.'

'I'm not. It has great investment potential.' She looked around the living room, her eyes slowly scanning over the furniture and the storage. 'You see if there's anything we missed. I wanted to look at the place without an agent gawking over my shoulder.'

'Sure.'

Sandy moved into the bedroom. He kept his laptop in his room. He hoped Ebony had done the same thing. He opened the drawers in the bedside tables looking for it, but instead found Ebony's stash of filled notebooks. There were two in the top drawer and two in the other. 'How am I going to get them out?'

'Find anything?' Tomy called out from the living room.

'Not yet.'

While he pondered how to get the notebooks out of the apartment without Tomy seeing, Sandy got down on his hands and knees and looked under the bed. Voila, the laptop. Another layer of problems. This was too big to put down his pants. He put the notebooks under the bed with the laptop, pushed them out of view and into the dust bunnies that inhabited the space, and then stood up as Tomy came in.

'Still nothing?' she asked.

He shook his head. 'What are we even looking for?'

She shrugged. They left the apartment and made their way down to the car.

'I'll run the key into the agent, so you don't have to turn off the car,' Sandy said helpfully as Tomy pulled up in front of the real estate agent's office.

'Great, thanks.' She handed Sandy an envelope with the agent's name on it.

Sandy smiled sweetly at the receptionist, a young man in his early twenties, while he put Tomy's envelope in his pocket. He looked over the receptionist's head, turning his own on its side as he read the signage on the back wall. 'Oops. Wrong agent. I am so sorry.' He walked back to the car.

'All good?'

Sandy nodded. Now he had to get into Ebony's place and return the key to the agent before they missed it.

'You okay?' Tomy asked when they were walking back to their desks.

'No. Feel a bit off actually. That's why I was so long in the toilet earlier. Might go home. I'll let the Sarge know.'

'Sure. Take care of yourself,' Tomy said as she sat behind the pile of paperwork on her desk.

———

sandy parked in the laneway at the back of the apartment building and raced up the stairs to Ebony's apartment, missing every second step. Pleased he wasn't panting when he got to her door, he unlocked it, closed it quietly behind him, and headed to the bedroom. He pulled out the laptop and notebooks, as well as some dust bunnies who wanted a change of scenery, bundled them into his arms and locked the door behind him.

The same receptionist sat behind the desk. Sandy thought quickly, 'Hi, I was in earlier.'

'I remember,' the young man scowled.

'You are not the wrong agent, after all. Silly me. Please give this envelope to the person whose name is on the front.'

The receptionist took the envelope, looked from it to Sandy, put it in a drawer, and pumped hand sanitizer onto his hands from the bottle on his desk.

'Oh, okay then,' Sandy said, reaching over to use the sanitizer. 'Can't be too careful, can we?' He chuckled to himself as he walked to his car. Before starting the ignition, he called Brad, who didn't answer. *Unusual.*

14

BRAD

The sun was dropping on the other side of the bay when I left my townhouse. If I were being watched, I should have been able to pick out a tail while driving to Ebony's. I had toyed with the idea of getting a tram to the city, catching a train to Altona, then a taxi to Ebony's, but that was tempting fate. If they were following me, suspicions would've been rampant if I got on a tram, let alone caught a train. As far as they knew, Ebony was dead. My friend, Sherryn Forbes was renting my duplex in Altona, and I was visiting.

I navigated the traffic to get out of the city and onto the Westgate Freeway. I use the term "freeway" lightly. In all the years I've driven on it, I would never have called it a freeway. This evening was no exception. But thanks to the peak hour traffic gods, there were no crashes to slow things up even more. My mobile connected to my car as soon as I turned on the ignition and I pressed the icon to call Sandy. I was in my townhouse when he called earlier, and I didn't answer. Free to talk now, I waited for him to pick up.

'Sorry about earlier. I think they bugged my house,

and I didn't want to speak to you and let anything slip. Did you get the stuff?'

'Hello, Brad. Yes, I'm fine, thank you. Even though I told a furphy at work so I could leave early to get the *stuff* you wanted.'

'I know you love me, and now I love you, too. Tell me how you got it and what it is.'

'I let the dust bunnies go. I released them. They seemed happy,' Sandy said when he finished his story.

'What?'

'Nothing.'

'I'm on my way to see Ebony, but I'll swing past your place first. Thanks.'

Sandy had two glasses and a bottle of red on the kitchen bench with some cheese, biscuits, and dip, set out on a nice plate.

'Expecting someone?' I asked, pulling out a stool and pouring wine into the two glasses.

'Yes. Someone to talk to, someone to share stories about my day with. Instead, I have you.'

We clinked glasses and said "cheers" before tasting the wine.

'Nice drop. Where did you get it?'

'Some dickhead gave it to me for my birthday six months ago, and hasn't been here since to help me drink it.'

'More fool him,' I said, putting my glass on the bench. 'It's been hectic. I'm sorry I've neglected you.'

Sandy's friendship is more important to me than anything else, even Ebony and her wellbeing. I had to make it up to him.

Sandy shrugged. 'Where is Ebony?'

'I can't tell you that. If I tell you, I really will have to kill you. She's safe. A new identity, the works.'

'She can't be far if you came here on your way.' Sandy sipped the wine, looking at my face contort from composure to insecurity.

'No wonder you made detective,' I quipped.

Sandy gulped the last of the wine from his glass, glared at me, daring me to have a go at him for treating the nectar of the gods with such contempt, and headed to his bedroom. I poured us both another glass and spread some Brie on a biscuit.

'Nice cheese,' I said, helping myself to some more.

Sandy came out with the laptop, put it on the bench, and went back for the notebooks.

'Thanks.'

'Aren't you going to open any of them?'

'I don't think so. And I don't know the laptop password.'

'There isn't one,' Sandy said.

I could feel my face redden — anger I could not control. 'Tell me you didn't turn it on.'

'Okay. I won't.' He moved to the other side of the bench and took a mouthful of wine.

'Why would you do that?'

'I'm a detective.'

'And?'

'There are new emails, but I didn't open any of them.'

'Shit, Sandy. The arsehole attaches a delivered and read receipt to the emails he sends her.'

'I saw those. I turned it off when I saw them.'

'But did you click "no," or whatever it asked when it the sender wanted a delivered receipt?'

'No.'

'We're stuffed. You'll have to destroy it. If he gets a delivered receipt he'll know someone has opened the email.'

'Stop being a drama queen. I'll take it to the office, store it there. It's part of the investigation. I have the right to look at it. Now all I have to do is explain to Tomy how I got it. This gets worse and worse. I don't think I need you as a friend anymore.'

I picked up the notebooks and put them in a small backpack Sandy gave me. 'I love you too. Thanks, mate. See you soon.'

———

I was pretty certain, but not one hundred percent, that they had not followed me, so I put the backpack on, put my jacket over the top and walked to my car. It wasn't as hard as I thought to keep the front of my body facing the street. I opened the passenger door and took off my jacket and the backpack in one fell swoop, throwing them onto the floor. I sauntered around to the driver's side, got in, and called Ebony.

'Hi. If the traffic has died down, I should be there in about thirty minutes.'

Silence

'Hello?'

'I don't think I want you to come over, Brad.' Her voice had a determined timbre to it. Strong. Forceful.

'Oh. Okay. I have your notebooks.'

More silence. This was nerve-wracking.

'All right. But I don't want you to stay the night.'

'Sure,' I said, pulling a face that not even a mother could love.

———

The garage door opened as soon as my car was in the driveway. I'd had it linked when I bought the place and never changed it. I don't think the tenants who had lived there for the last couple of years would have appreciated that. 'Oh well. Works for me now.'

15

EBONY

Ebony heard the garage door open, annoyed that another level of privacy was breached. She would wait and see if Brad knocked on the connecting door before letting her temper get the better of her.

The knock was loud enough to be heard all through the house. She let him wait. His second knock was more forceful. She opened the door.

'Hi,' he said, moving to embrace her.

She stepped back. 'Shut the door behind you, please.'

'Sure.' He followed her to the downstairs living room. 'Something wrong?'

'I've been thinking about my life, and I don't see you fitting into it.'

Brad lowered himself onto the couch and looked through the French doors to the beautifully designed alfresco area. He didn't respond to Ebony's statement. She could see enough of his face to realise he was in pain: his mouth pointed down at the corners, his cheeks were flushed, and the eye she could see was filling with tears. This wasn't the hired assassin who sat opposite her in the café all those weeks ago. This was a man who had lost his way and thought she was the one to steer him in the right direction.

'You don't need me, Brad,' she said sitting on the armchair to his left.

He turned to look at her, sorrow etched in the furrows on his forehead, the creases around his eyes, and the corners of his mouth.

'Yes. I do. What has brought you to this decision?'

'I spent the day getting to know the neighbourhood, picturing me living in it. I didn't see you in that picture.' She didn't tell him about her decision not to stay.

'I'll go then. I have your notebooks. I'll get them out of the car.'

She stayed in the armchair while he went to his car, coming back in with the bundle of notebooks that contained her life's work.

'Thank you,' Ebony said as Brad handed her the treasure. 'You don't have to go. I've cooked dinner. There's enough for the two of us.'

'I don't want to intrude. You deserve your space. I'll see you another time.'

'Brad!' Ebony raised her voice. 'Please stay for dinner. We can talk.'

He looked as if his mind was torn between two choices: one good, one evil. 'I don't want to intrude. Seems I've done quite a bit of that, giving no consideration to you and what you need or want.'

'Thank you for recognising that,' Ebony said, putting the notebooks on the coffee table. 'Let's have a drink and I'll serve dinner.'

'This is very good,' Brad said, as Ebony put a second helping of paella on his plate. 'You are vegetarian. What did you use instead of chorizo?'

'If I tell you that, I will have to kill you,' Ebony said, sitting down opposite him to finish her meal.

'Funny, that's what I said to Sandy earlier when he asked where you were.'

Ebony could feel her face flush. Comments like this one brought back the reality of her situation.

'Does he know my new name?'

'Of course not. I have to protect you both. All he knows is that you are safe. He doesn't need to know anymore.'

Ebony collected her notebooks from the coffee table, moved her dinner plate to the bench, and set the books in order in front of her.

'Do you want some help to go through them?' Brad asked hopefully.

'Maybe. For now, I'm just going to skim through them to remind myself what's in each one. Do you want to make coffee?'

Brad nodded.

'Sandy got the books for you,' he said as he put Ebony's coffee in front of her. 'He got the laptop too, but he's taking that to his office.'

'Why?'

'Because he opened your email program, and the one highlighted popped up saying it asked for a delivery and read receipt.'

'Oh Brad, that email was probably from your father's publishing company. I don't know if Sophie is a real person anymore, or if it is him pretending to be someone else.'

Ebony's hands started shaking and her face lost its colour.

'It's okay, Ebony,' Brad reassured. 'Sandy has a

right to look at your computer for the investigation. It won't matter.'

'Are you sure?'

Brad got up from the table and moved around to the other side to sit next to her. 'Yes. I am sure.'

'Thanks. I changed the password on my Microsoft account the other day using the phone you gave me. Just as well. When they get into the laptop, they won't be able to access my OneDrive or Google Drive, that's where all my work is. In fact, he shouldn't have been able to get into my email.'

'Oh, I'll ask him about it. Maybe it was an old email. I have something else to tell you. In a visit to my father, he let it slip that he had spoken to your mother. He knows about the notebooks.'

Ebony got up from the table and walked toward the French doors. 'Just as I think I'm getting back to my old self and making plans, something like this happens. I hate my life.'

Brad moved toward her.

'Please go,' she said. 'I want to be alone. I'll call you tomorrow. You can see yourself out.'

Ebony stared through the glass while Brad made his way back to the garage. She let the tears flow, let the heartbreak swallow her.

16

BRAD

My father's summons was terse, as usual. Not a phone call, a text. I could feel the malice in his words just by reading them. His domination of my life was pushing me to the edge.

I shoved Accessory Ninety-Eight out of the way — I'd long since lost count of the new faces that greeted me each time I made this trek. While he pushed the button to call the elevator, I scurried for the stairwell.

He called after me. 'You have to come back,' he wailed.

I almost felt sorry for him. It only took a few minutes for me to get to the third floor, but realised I would have to do something about my fitness when Accessory Ninety-Eight was waiting at the top of the stairs, arms folded across his chest, face as red as my father's company logo that was on his shirt. Again I pushed past him, attempting to stride confidently into my father's office. The panting took away from my bravado somewhat.

'I have assistants for a reason,' my father bellowed. 'Don't do that again.'

I couldn't be bothered arguing with him, so I sat down, waiting for his tirade. He stared at me.

'What? What do you want, Father? I have a business to run.'

'Where are the notebooks?'

'SHIT!' I screamed at him. 'I've done my job. You find the notebooks.'

'Someone has her laptop,' my father sneered. 'Could be the same people who have the notebooks.'

'Could be,' I answered, keeping the anger foremost in my voice. 'You find out who has the laptop and send them a nicely worded card asking for the notebooks.'

'Do you have the notebooks, Junior?'

I'm not a fan of telling lies. I am happy enough to deceive someone (like my father) if it helps another person, but lying to his face doesn't sit well. Glad I didn't have to lie.

'No. I do not have the notebooks.' I thought I answered convincingly. I would know in a second or two.

'You did have them, though. Didn't you?'

Quick thinking was required—not uncommon when dealing with him. 'Did I? Well, if you are so sure I had them, you must know where they are?'

He stiffened, glaring at me with those eyes. 'Does Sanderson have them? With the laptop?'

It was my turn to stiffen, but I gathered my thoughts in an instant. He often used this trick to glean information, confusing his target into thinking he already knew what he wanted to hear.

'Ask him,' I countered. 'Until you told me about the notebooks, which you learned about during a conversation with Miss Makepeace's mother, I did not know of their existence.'

I watched him process the fact that I had remembered he had spoken to Ebony's mother. 'Is that all? I'm busy.'

'Why are you spending so much time at your place in Altona? I thought you had tenants in it?'

Was there nothing off limits to this monster?

'My tenants moved out. I have a friend living there. She needed a place to stay—short term—I offered it to her.'

'Who is she?'

'What business is that of yours? I don't follow you around trying to find out who you're screwing physically and metaphorically. So keep your goons out of my life. She's a friend. I've known her for a long time. Do you know what friends are?'

'I don't appreciate your tone, Junior,' he snarled.

I hit a soft spot there. No friends. Make a note.

'So you summoned me here to ask me about some notebooks. Could you not have done that over the phone?'

'I prefer to ask questions in person. Gives me a chance to judge a person's face. I'm an excellent judge of whether someone is lying.'

'Good skill to have,' I snarled. 'Anything else?'

'You seem to be coping with the fallout of the tasks I gave you, namely Steven and Miss Makepeace. It's apparent your conscience does not bother you. That's good. I will have another job for you soon. Don't be a stranger.'

With that, he dismissed me.

My heart threatened to leap out of my chest it was thumping so rapidly.

What did he want me to do next?

17

EBONY

Ebony sat on the outdoor couch on the upstairs balcony looking over the Norfolk Island Pines to the bay. The notebooks were next to her. She hadn't looked at them since Brad left last night, deciding to dedicate the morning to poring over their pages. But she would finish her coffee first and take in the view's serenity.

From where she sat, the sea looked like a sheet of blue Perspex: flat, serene, unmoving. The pines, usually being jostled by a sea breeze at the very least, were holding their own. There were container ships off in the distance that looked as if painted onto the background. She couldn't tell if they were moving.

Picking up the first book on the pile, she wondered if it had been difficult for Detective Sanderson to get them out of her apartment. She felt guilty for sending Brad away last night when he and Sanderson had gone to such trouble for her.

'Yes, but he is the one who "killed" me,' she said aloud.

She put the book to her face, smelling its familiar smell—the smell of her old apartment North Melbourne. The one she had almost paid off. The one her parents would now sell and, after paying off the rest of the loan, would have a tidy sum to spend on holidays, a caravan, whatever. With the enumerations of her finances, Ebony remembered her life assurance: a one million dollar policy in favour of her parents. *Goodness, they will be set up.*

She put down her coffee mug and opened a notebook. It was the first one she'd started five years ago; she smiled at the hurried hand that tried to get thoughts onto paper before they evaporated from her mind. The ideas that filled the pages never made it into her novels.

But I might refer to these again later. I can develop the concepts, the characters.

By the second notebook she had taken to writing in pencil. Bemused by her aversion to taking notes on the computer, Ebony read the words as if for the first time, as if someone else had written them. Most of the ramblings had made their way into her first two novels —the first two Brad's father published. She shuddered and a thread of worry weaved its way into her mind. Was he a real publisher, were her books worthy?

Hearing her stomach rumble, Ebony looked at her phone for the time. The morning had evaporated. She picked up the notebooks and stashed them in a storage box under the bed. Closing the French doors on the balcony, she made her way downstairs to get something to eat. Glancing at her reflection in the bathroom mirror as she walked past, it horrified her to see she was still in her pyjamas. The morning really had disappeared.

———

Ebony made a cheese, lettuce, and tomato sandwich with mayonnaise. She put it in a food container, took a bottle of sugar free drink out of the fridge (Brad really had thought of everything) grabbed the front door key from the hook in the pantry, and headed for the beach. As she closed the door, she thought again about the feasibility of getting a dog, then reminded herself that she was not staying.

The foreshore was busier this afternoon. The day had warmed markedly once the morning cloud cleared, and Ebony reminded herself how much she loved spring. Her grandmother would say on days like this that you wouldn't want to be dead for quids. No. Ebony didn't want to be dead. But she was.

The reminder splashed a swirl of grey on her sunny afternoon. She slipped off her sandals, feeling the sand between her toes, and avoided the dried up seaweed as she walked next to the retaining wall looking for a place to sit. The seagulls squawked and pecked each other before she had the sandwich out of the container.

'You're not getting any,' she yelled at them.

'That's selfish,' a male voice admonished.

Ebony jumped and knocked the plastic bottle of drink onto the sand. Before she bent to pick it up, she looked behind to see who spoke. Detective Sanderson stood on the footpath side of the retaining wall. Ebony felt the colour drain from her face, but she did not speak to him. Pulling her hat a bit further onto her head and adjusting her sunglasses, she turned away and nibbled on her sandwich.

'Oh, okay then,' the detective said, moving off along the footpath.

She was sure the kids splashing around in the

shallows could hear the breath she let out. 'Breathe, breathe,' she told herself. 'I am in disguise.' That the detective seemed not to have recognised her was no consolation to Ebony. *Why is he here?*

Still munching on her sandwich, trying to appear as nonchalant as her nerves would allow, Ebony looked to her left, watching Sanderson. He walked along the footpath and stopped outside her place. Well, Brad's place. He stood for a few moments, checked the traffic, and crossed the road. Walking to the front door, it looked as if he pressed the doorbell and stood back, waiting for someone to appear.

If she had been home, would she have opened the door? She had a new name and a new look. No. She would never answer the door.

He stood for a minute, then pressed the doorbell button again. The dog a couple of doors down barked in annoyance. Again, he waited a minute, but walked away when the bell went unanswered. She saw him cross the road and make his way back to where she was sitting. She picked up the drink bottle and dragging her feet in the sand, made her way toward the water's edge. Her feet sunk into the wet sand as the waves lapped around her ankles. 'I hope he goes away before the tide comes in,' she mumbled.

So her feet wouldn't freeze, she walked along the water's edge until she thought Sanderson had left. She couldn't see him.

The sand stuck to her wet feet as she made her way up to the retaining wall and onto the footpath on the other side of it. She brushed the sand off her feet as best she could, put her sandals on and headed away from the house, crossing the road further down. She would go back the long way, around the side streets. She had to be sure he'd left.

———

Her hand shook as she unlocked the front door, glad to have it shut behind her. With sand on her feet she would have preferred to go in through the garage, but fear and dread had her picturing Sanderson creeping up behind her and getting into the garage before she had time to hit the remote to close the door. She stood against the wall for a few moments, controlling her breathing.

She tiptoed down the hallway to the laundry and threw her sandals in the sink. Grabbing a towel, she wiped the now dry sand off her feet, telling herself she would clean it up later. Now she wanted to sit down and have a glass of wine, something to calm her nerves.

What was supposed to be a sip turned into a glass.

She poured herself another and called Brad.

18

SANDERSON (SANDY)

'Where have you been?' Detective Tomy asked her partner when he finally answered his phone. She'd been trying to reach him on and off all morning.

'I had a dentist's appointment. Didn't I tell you?'

'No, you didn't. And you didn't tell Sarge either. She's not impressed.'

'Weird. I thought I'd said something. Can you cover for me until I get in? I'll be about 30 minutes.'

'Hurry,' Tomy growled before hanging up.

———

After Sandy had grovelled to the Sergeant he tried to do the same with Tomy. She brushed him aside and asked him what the dentist did.

'Nothing today. I have to go back next week to have my teeth cleaned and a filling. No more jam on my toast.' He grinned at Tomy, whose expression did not change.

'So you would have had a thirty-minute appointment today. That explains why you were MIA for three hours. Make sure you let Sarge know about your next dentist's appointment,' she said using her fingers to show double quotation marks around dentist. 'And put it in the diary so I won't have to work myself into a state trying to get hold of you.'

'I'm sorry. What was so urgent?'

'I had a look at Miss Makepeace's laptop.'

Sandy swallowed hard. 'Did you find anything?'

'Yes. As a matter of fact, I did. Someone has changed her passwords so we can't get into her emails, or her cloud storage. Thoughts?'

'I don't have any,' Sandy said, shaking his head.

'That's not unusual, is it? You not having any thoughts. At least of late.'

Sandy pulled out his chair and sat at his desk. Looking at Tomy, he asked if she had got into any older emails.

'No. The password has changed; we can't look at any.'

'How do you know the password has changed?' Sandy asked, genuinely confused. 'When I turn on my laptop and go to my email program, it starts straight away.'

'When you said once that you weren't great with computers, you weren't joking, were you?'

'No.'

'Listen carefully. Once you are in the computer and start programs, they automatically fire up. The only reason they won't is if there's been a glitch some-where, or you have changed the password.'

'How do you know there hasn't been a glitch then?' Sandy rubbed his chin. He really was confused. 'Or maybe Miss Makepeace changed the password herself before he shot her.'

Tomy ignored his comment. 'I'm taking it to IT.

They might find a way in. I have a nagging feeling that whoever killed our writer communicated with her, possibly via email. Did we ever find her mobile?'

Sandy took a deep breath, relieved that he could answer Tomy without lying to her. 'Yes, it's in the evidence room. Do you want me to get it?'

'Sure. That would be great. Make sure it's charged,' she sniggered, picking up the laptop and heading to the stairwell.

After signing the paperwork, Sandy walked back to his desk with Ebony's mobile phone in hand. Finding the on switch, he held it down, waiting for the phone to fire up. It didn't. Flat.

'Does anyone have a charger for an old Samsung?' he called over the other heads in the office.

'They all fit,' a voice answered. 'They're not like the other one. The same charger fits all the older models.'

'Do you have one?' Sandy repeated.

'Yep.' His colleague put the charger on Sandy's desk. 'Don't forget to give it back to me.'

While plugged in to the charger, the phone would be useable. Sandy tried the on button again. The phone lit up, lights flashed across the screen, and then it demanded a password.

'Anything?' Tomy asked, pulling up her chair.

'Where's the laptop?'

'With IT. Did you think they could do it instantly? Yeah, not so much. What's happening with the phone?'

'I've plugged it in, but it wants a password,' Sandy said, staring at the phone's unresponsive screen.

'I'll call her friend, Gabrielle. She might know. They were pretty close.'

'How do you know how close they were?'

'Detective work. You know that thing that you used to be okay at, and now you suck?'

'You sound like a friend of mine, Tomy. It's annoying.'

Sandy stared at Ebony's phone while Tomy tried to reach Gabrielle.

'Good news,' she yelled in his ear. 'She's going to text me a list of combinations of numbers Ebony may have used. Good work, Tomy,' she said, patting herself on the back.

Sandy read the first possible password to Tomy, and she tapped it in. Rejection. The second possibility was rejected. She keyed in the third possible combination but stopped short of hitting the arrow key to progress.

'What's wrong?' Sandy asked.

'What if it locks us out after three tries? We'll be well and truly stuffed then. I'd better take this to IT, too.'

Tomy pushed her chair over as she stood up. 'Oops. Get that for me.' She hurried to the stairwell.

'Rude,' he called after her.

———

Sandy was poring over the notes relating to a real homicide when Tomy thumped back into the room.

'You've been gone a while. I've been trying to reach you,' he said sarcastically.

'Funny. I waited for IT to look at the phone. They got into it. The numeric password is—wait for it—4, 3, 2, 1.'

'Not very secure,' Sandy commented.

'No, not really. Anyway, let's have a look at her messages to see if we can find anything of interest.'

'Does her email come through on her phone?'.

'Good call, Sandy.'

This was as nice as she'd been to him all day. 'Thanks.'

Tomy played with Ebony's phone looking for the email icon. Finding it, she tapped and waited. 'Nope. It's asking for a password. Shit.'

She put the phone on the desk between them, and tapped the messages icon, scrolling through at such a rate that Sandy felt dizzy.

'Slow down. I can't focus.'

'Seriously? Maybe you should go to the optometrist when you've finished at the dentist.'

Stopping suddenly, Tomy gasped. 'There's a message here from Sapphire Publishing, but it hasn't been opened.'

'Is that her publisher?'

Tomy nodded. 'It asks her to call them. Apologising that they usually communicate via email, but it's important that they speak to her. The person's name is Sophie. It's dated the day Ebony was shot.'

19

BRAD

Ebony's rejection left me feeling, well, rejected. I'm not used to that feeling. Usually I am the one doing the rejecting. That's why my personal assistant is a bloke. He's not a blokey bloke, but he's not a woman either. He's not likely to be rejected by me.

While I was thinking about last night's sad state of affairs, my mobile rang. I had changed the ringtone to the theme song from the Addams Family. The lyrics reminded me of my family, creepy, mysterious. I let the first verse play before I checked the screen. It was Ebony.

'Hi,' I said, trying not to sound too excited to hear from her. Rejection leaves a sour taste.

'Hi, Brad. Something scary has happened.'

'What? Are you okay?'

My heart beat faster than I would have liked. It was pounding in my ears.'

'Yes. Detective Sanderson was here. He spoke to me on the beach, but I don't think he recognised me. He knocked on the front door of the house and hung around for a while before leaving.'

'That doesn't make sense,' I said, more to myself than to Ebony.

'I know. I thought you said he was in on the plan.'

'He is. Leave it with me. Do you want me to come over later? Or now?'

'Could you come now, please? I'm quite shaken up.'

I wanted to ask her how long I could stay, and I was annoyed that I could enter the premises when it suited her. But I didn't.

'I'll be there soon.'

———

She put her arms around me as soon as I stepped into the hallway from the garage. She had been crying. I told her it would be okay, and led her to the couch, the one that faced outside onto the beautifully manicured small garden and alfresco. We sat together; she leaned into me. I could feel her heart thumping. I put my arm around her and kissed her forehead.

I waited. No point in hurrying her. *She'll tell me all about it when she's ready.*

'Aren't you going to ask me what happened?' she threw at me, pushing herself away from my embrace.

Can't win.

'I thought I'd leave it to you to begin when you're ready. But okay, tell me what happened.'

Ebony relayed the story about the lovely morning sitting on the balcony and starting to look through the notebooks, to packing a sandwich and a drink and walking over the road to the beach, setting herself up on the sand leaning against the retaining wall. I let her continue, but wanted desperately to ask if she found anything of interest in the notebooks. She finished with the walk around the side streets and letting herself in.

'Any idea why he would be here?' she asked

I shook my head. 'Are you sure he didn't recognise you?'

'He didn't. I was wearing sunglasses and a hat, and apart from my yelling at the birds, he didn't hear me speak.'

I frowned, thoughts racing through my head like greyhounds around a track. Sandy was clearly looking for Ebony, but why?

We sat next to each other, gazing through the French doors, deep in thought. She had moved in close again when my phone startled us both.

'Is that the Addams Family?'

'Yes. I think it is fitting,' I said.

'Indeed.' A wry smile took over her face.

I looked at the screen. 'It's Sandy. This will be interesting.'

'Sandy, hello,' I said into the phone.

'I wasn't expecting that,' he said. 'You're usually rude.'

'Am I? No. I'm not. But I can be.'

He ignored me. 'Are you busy? Want to catch up for a beer?'

'Sure. Claude's in an hour.' I hung up without waiting for him to respond.

Ebony looked at me. I want to say questioningly, but it was more than that. Her eyes were red from crying, her lips dry, and her cheeks flushed, and her expression was a mixture of concern, fear of the unknown, and dread. I wanted to see a glimmer of "hug me, Brad," but that wasn't there. I looked hard enough.

'He wants to catch up for a beer,' I said unnecessarily. Ebony would have gathered that from my curt responses to my friend.

'Will you come straight back here after you've finished talking to him?'

'I would like to,' I said hopefully. 'But it will depend on what he has to say. I'm not concerned about my father and his cronies finding out a woman lives here—you are no longer Ebony Makepeace—but what Sandy says will impact lots of things.'

'I think I will need some company tonight, Brad,' she said, those big brown eyes penetrating my outer defences, like they did the day I shot her.

Awkward. All by itself, with a mind of its own, my willy reacted. In one movement, I leaned in to kiss her and pulled a cushion over my lap. If she realised what was happening, she let it pass. Too many other things on her mind for now.

———

As usual, I arrived before Sandy and was shown to a table by the window. I'd be able to see him arrive if I wanted to. I didn't. I ordered a drink without waiting for him. Wine wasn't going to cut it tonight. I ordered a beer. I took the last gulp as he walked in.

'Not waiting for me. What a surprise,' he sniped.

'I was thirsty.'

I ordered another drink when Sandy ordered his first. I waited for the server to move away before starting the conversation. 'What's up?'

'Do you have Ebony ensconced in your house in Altona?'

'Why? What difference does it make, and why do you need to know?' I sipped my drink, trying not to lean over and punch him in the face with my free hand. It stayed on my lap, fist clenched. Ready.

'I'm curious. I might need to ask her about her laptop and her phone.'

He was lying.

'She's dead.' I reminded him. 'So if you can't work out how to get into her laptop and her phone, that's your problem. Thought you were a detective.'

'It doesn't become you, Brad.'

'What doesn't?'

'Sarcasm.'

We knew each other well. I knew he was lying about Ebony's laptop and phone, and he knew I was evading the question.

'I'll ask you again,' I said, hoping to move the conversation along. 'Why do you care who is staying in my Altona house?'

'I don't, really. I just wanted to make sure that you had her securely tucked away. It was her I saw opening the door and letting herself in early today, wasn't it? The disguise is great though. It wasn't until I heard her speak that I was sure it was her. Until then, she was nobody.'

My patience was evaporating into the ether as quickly as my drink went down my gullet. 'Do you want anything to eat?' I asked, before continuing the conversation. Without waiting for his reply, I indicated to the server to come over and ordered two cheese and tomato toasted sandwiches.

'I don't want anything to eat,' Sandy said when the server left to process the order.

'I didn't order for you.' I was lying and he knew it. 'I'm hungry. Be straight with me, please.' I sat back in the chair, my left hand still on my lap, fist clenched. It matched my jaw.

'I had a call from your father.' He stared at me, obviously gauging my reaction to this bombshell.

'I don't understand,' I said through my further tightening jaw. He knows she is dead. He went to her funeral.'

'He did. If he were convinced, why did he call me?'

'I give up, Einstein,' I snapped. 'Why did he call you?'

'I think he suspects, Brad. And if that's the case, if I found her, he will too.'

The food arrived. The server put a plate in front of each of us, and as he left, I leaned over and grabbed the one in front of Sandy and put it next to mine. 'Told you I was hungry. I want to know exactly what he said to you. Start at the beginning.'

Sandy eyed the toasted sandwich and looked at me. I pushed a plate back in front of him. He took a bite, chewed, swallowed. Made me hang until he was ready.

'He greeted me politely and asked if I remembered him. I told him I did. He asked how the investigation into Ebony's murder was going.'

'What did you say?'

'I was caught off guard. Couldn't remember if I was supposed to know he owned the publishing company, so I played dumb at first. I asked him what interest he had in the case. He said he was her publisher and wondered if I would avenge her death. That took me back a bit. Avenged was an odd word to use. I told him the case was progressing. He was quiet for a few seconds, and then asked if we found anything on her laptop, adding that he was waiting for a book from her. I told him I wasn't at liberty to say what we had or hadn't found. That didn't stop him. He asked if we found any notebooks in her apartment because she planned out her novels in them.

'It was all a bit much. If I wasn't in on this, if he'd called Tomy instead of me, her senses would have worked overtime and he would be down as a suspect.'

'That might have been a better outcome,' I said, finishing half of the sandwich. 'None of what he asked shows that he thinks she is still alive, Sandy. He's fishing, he is after the notebooks, and the laptop if he can get it. Don't be surprised if the next call you get is from her mother asking about the same things. He'll work on her grief and manipulate her. That's what he does.'

'Sorry, Brad. I've never covered up a pretend murder before.'

'All good. But don't go to the house again. It's not appreciated.'

'If you think it's all under control, I'll leave it at that,' Sandy said, wiping his face with a serviette.

We finished our sandwiches, had a coffee each, and my fist and jaw unclenched.

The arsehole won't give up.

20

EBONY

Brad called Ebony to let her know he was on the way back and asked if she wanted him to pick up something for her dinner. She didn't.

He knocked on the door between the garage and the house and waited for her to acknowledge him. She called out for him to come in.

'I appreciate you knocking. Thank you,' she said as he made his way to the living room. She was curled up in an armchair watching something on the television that he didn't recognise. 'What did he have to say?' she asked.

'He overreacted to a phone call. My father called him and asked how the investigation was going. Said he wondered if Sandy had found your laptop and notebooks. Of course, Sandy told him nothing. It was a fishing expedition. He wants your notebooks, and we need to find out why. I told Sandy he would probably hear from your mother next. My father will manipulate her into trying to get more information.'

'That doesn't explain why Sandy was here today,' Ebony said, moving to sit next to Brad on the couch.

'He panicked. As he said, he's never covered up a pretend murder before.'

'Do you think they followed him here?' Ebony's face showed signs of desperation.

'Even if they did, doesn't matter. My father knows I've got this place, and he really thinks you are dead. The only reason he would have anyone followed is to see if they lead him to your notebooks. It's like a treasure hunt for him.'

She put her head on Brad's shoulder and sat quietly for a few minutes. He didn't move or speak again.

'I'm lonely,' she said, looking at him.

'Do you want me to stay here more often?'

'I'll think about it. When I'm writing, I don't need company during the day, but I'm not writing.'

'Well, there's no reason you can't write. Especially if it makes you happy,' Brad soothed. 'Maybe we could start with the notebooks. They might inspire you.'

'Funny you should say that, there were some notes on stories I hadn't yet developed in the notebook I looked through this morning. I'll get it.'

Ebony brought two notebooks downstairs and sat in the armchair with them on her lap. She looked across at Brad and asked him if he would like to go through the one she had in the morning, and she would start on the other one.

They sat quietly. The only noise in the comfortable space was the turning of pages.

———

Fascinated with Ebony's ability to capture the essence of people she observed, Brad kept looking over at her, imagining her in that café surreptitiously watching people come and go, incorporating them into her stories. He didn't read every word, instead used his index finger to skim along the lines of writing.

'I found nothing in this one,' Brad said, closing the notebook and standing up to stretch. 'Mind if I put the kettle on?'

'No. Go for it. I'll have a peppermint tea, please.' Ebony hadn't taken her eyes off the pages she was reading.

Bringing over the cup of tea and some biscuits he unearthed in the pantry, Brad asked if Ebony had found anything.

'No. I'll start on another one tomorrow.' She sat back in the armchair, legs tucked underneath her, holding the mug of tea with both hands. 'Do you want to stay the night?'

Brad nodded, holding his own cup of tea and looking over the top of it at her.

'I thought we were finished,' Brad said, as he followed Ebony up the stairs, his heart pounding in anticipation.

''So did I. but there's something reassuring about you, even though you tried to kill me.'

'I didn't try to kill you,' Brad corrected. 'I saved you.' He sat on the end of the bed watching her close the blinds.

She walked over to him, the throbbing between her legs increasing with each step. Her brain told her this was a bad idea. He wasn't right for her. He was twisted, weird, odd. And his father was a psychopath. But the pounding in her chest, the tingle when he touched her, forced her brain to get out of the way. She wanted him.

As he unbuttoned her jeans and pulled them

down, she wondered if she really wanted him, or just the sex. When he leaned forward and gently manipulated her undies down while kissing her abdomen, she knew it was him.

21

SANDERSON (SANDY)

Sandy checked the number on his mobile before answering. He didn't know it, but swiped to answer anyway.

'Detective Sanderson?' the woman asked.

'Speaking.'

'Detective Sanderson, my name is Julia Makepeace. Ebony's mother.'

Sandy swallowed, then shook his head. 'How may I help you, Mrs Makepeace?'

'Ebony's publisher has been in touch with me, and he is very eager to get hold of Ebony's notebooks. I know she had a few. She planned her novels in them. Only she could understand the scribblings, but Mr Culley is thinking of publishing her last book posthumously, and he thought the notebooks might add some light into how she planned it. She'd emailed the draft to his office a couple of days before she was shot.'

Sandy gave the woman a chance to take a breath. He heard wavering in her voice. 'We don't have them, Mrs Makepeace. As I told Mr Culley, we have her laptop and her phone, but we didn't come across any notebooks in her apartment. I can't help you.'

He heard her sniff. 'Oh, that is so disappointing. To publish Ebony's last book would be a fitting tribute to her. Could you please look in her apartment again? If not, I'll ask her friend Gabrielle to search for them.'

'We will look again for you, Mrs Makepeace.'

'Oh, thank you so much, Detective Sanderson. We'll speak again soon.' She hung up.

He looked at the screen of his phone, deciding whether to add her number to his contacts. They had her landline number. Why did he need her mobile too? He cleared the screen.

Tomy arrived carrying a tray holding two takeaway cups. Sandy desperately hoped one of them was a cup of coffee for him.

'Good morning, Tomy,' he said brightly. 'I just had a weird phone call.'

Tomy handed Sandy one of the cups. 'Two sugars. You're welcome.'

He smiled at her, thanking her for being so thoughtful and took a sip. It was just the right temperature and glided down his throat. He put his head back, enjoying the sensation.

'You were saying something about a phone call?' Tomy asked.

'Remember, I told you the other day how Ebony Makepeace's publisher called about her notebooks?'

Tomy nodded.

'The mother called just now, insisting we look in Ebony's apartment again to find them. Gave me some yarn about publishing her daughter's last book. Feels off to me.'

'Feels off to me, too.' Tomy said. 'Do you think we should put the publisher on our list of suspects?'

Sandy stopped himself from choking on the coffee. 'Sure. Why not?'

'I don't think we need to bother going back to the victim's apartment. We've been there a dozen times and haven't found the notebooks.' Tomy threw her empty coffee cup into the bin and waited for a response from Sandy.

'I agree,' he said, relief washing over him like water from a showerhead.

'But,' Tomy continued, 'what do we know about the publisher?'

Sandy shrugged. 'Have you heard from IT? We might find something in the emails.'

Tomy stood and made her way to the stairwell. 'I'll hassle them.'

While she was away, Sandy called Brad, who didn't answer. He left a message saying the mother had called badgering about the notebooks, but Tomy didn't want to go back to the apartment to look for them.

'Your father is now officially a suspect,' Sandy said before hanging up.

Tomy walked back into the office, laptop under her arm. 'They got in,' she said. The grin reminded Sandy of a child opening a present on their birthday.

Setting the laptop down on the desk between them, Tomy opened it and turned it on. A picture of Ebony, Gabrielle, and James took up the screen.

'It's sad when you see this type of thing,' Tomy said. 'There she is with her friends, happy, no idea what was coming.'

'That's the same for all of us,' Sandy murmured. 'We don't know what is ahead.'

'Yes, but most of us don't end up dead at the hands of a murderous villain.'

Sandy swallowed hard. Brad wasn't a murderous villain. Far from it.

Tomy clicked on the email icon, and typed in the password the IT department had given her. The last email dated a day before Ebony died was from her bank telling her not to open suspect emails.

'Why do they do that? It's stupid. Sending you an email telling you not to open suspect emails.' Tomy shook her head and scrolled down the list slowly.

'Here's one from her publisher, a woman called Sophie. It's dated the day she was shot.' Tomy turned the laptop slightly so Sandy could see too.

'Seems that when Ebony didn't answer the text message, Sophie followed up with an email.'

> *Dear Ebony,*
>
> *Are you able to call me? I'd like to talk to you about the premise of the draft you sent us. Its contents perturbed my boss and he asked me to find out how you came up with the idea. He wants to see your notes.*
>
> *Cheers,*
> *Sophie Marris*
> *Sapphire Publishing*

'I'll look up their address. We're paying these people a visit.' Tomy closed Ebony's laptop, put it in her top drawer, locked it, and moved to the computer on her desk.

'I'll drive,' Tomy said to Sandy as they made their way to the building's basement car park. 'You navigate.'

'Isn't that what the GPS is for?'

'I don't trust it. You navigate.'

———

The address for Sapphire Publishing was on Exhibition Street in Melbourne, a few blocks from the Victoria Police building in Spencer Street. Sandy put the police parking permit on the dashboard of the unmarked car, as Tomy pulled into a loading zone.

'Bit of an ordinary address,' Tomy said, pressing the button on the remote to lock the car.

Sapphire Publishing was listed on the directory in the foyer as being on level three. While in the elevator, Sandy wondered how Brad's father would react if he saw him. He hoped he would pretend they had never met before; it would be too hard to explain to Tomy how he knew Mr Culley.

Two thugs dressed in black, the same height and build as each other, guarded the entrance to level three.

'They look like bookends,' Sandy whispered to Tomy.

She giggled while fishing around in her pocket for her police ID. 'Detective Tomy, this is Detective Sanderson.' She waited while Sandy got his ID out. 'We are here to see a person called Sophie.'

'You need an appointment,' the first thug growled.

'No. We don't actually,' Tomy said. 'Please tell Ms Marris we are here. And we'd like to wait inside, not out here in the hallway.'

'I'll be back in a moment,' the thug said while the other one folded his arms, blocking entrance to the office with his bulk.

'Let them pass,' thug numer one said to his partner. He opened the door for them, and the detectives stepped into the office space. Knowing how wealthy Brad's father was, the unpretentious decor astonished Sandy. No plush furniture or gaudy paintings, no lavish carpeting. Just the bare essentials required to run a business.

Brad's father came through a door on the other side of the office, hand outstretched, ready to greet Tomy. Sandy squirmed, but Culley ignored him.

'Detective Tomy, how nice to meet you. And you must be Detective Sanderson.' Culley looked at Sandy with no hint of recognition on his face. 'We spoke on the phone the other day, did we not?'

'Yes,' Sandy whispered.

Tomy took the lead in the questioning. 'Mr Culley, we would like to speak to Sophie Marris.'

'Why is that Detective Tomy?' Culley asked.

'It's between us and her. Part of the ongoing investigation into Miss Makepeace's murder.'

Sandy watched Culley's face for a sign of discomfort. None appeared.

'I'm afraid Sophie doesn't work here any longer. She left. Quite suddenly, too. Didn't even give her notice. Just emailed saying she wasn't coming back. Very unprofessional, she won't be getting a reference.'

'Oh. I see,' Tomy said.

Sandy knew from her tone that the only thing she saw was procrastination and obfuscation.

'No worries. If you could give us her contact details, we'll get out of your hair.'

'I would be more than happy to help you, Detective, but the computers are down, and we don't keep records on paper anymore.'

'When they are back up and running, please let

me know. It's important.' Tomy handed Culley her business card. 'Let's go,' she said to Sandy.

'What's the strategy?' Sandy asked when they were in the car.

'No point pushing him about the computers being down. We both know that's horseshit. All he's done is made me more determined to find this elusive Sophie. He's hiding something.'

22

BRAD

The only thing that could ruin the euphoric feeling that washed over me was hearing from my father. Ebony and I spent the night in each other's arms. And when I thought of the way she approached our love-making, my willy reacted.

Best not think about it.

Driving toward my townhouse so I could change into more appropriate business attire, I realised the phone dedicated to the arsehole, was ringing. I ignored it. He couldn't summon me into his presence if I didn't acknowledge him. He called again. I was proud of myself–first time for everything.

A text made its way to the screen, so I told Google to read it to me. "Answer your fucking phone. I want to see you. NOW."

I ignored the text and the next three phone calls. I have a business to run. My clients are important. It's the way I make a living independent of him.

After a quick shower and dressing in clothes to impress, I headed to my office. I greeted my personal assistant, Ferdinand, with a huge smile.

'Get some last night, did you?' he asked.

'Don't be rude.'

'It's what I do,' he said. 'By the way, there's some great big monster-looking fellow in your office. Wouldn't wait out here. Wouldn't follow my instructions. I'm losing my touch.'

I didn't respond. The monster would be one of Father's accessories, come to lay down the law.

'I'll keep it brief,' I said to Ferdinand. A pretentious name for a pretentious, but very efficient, person. 'Keep Dr Enfield entertained if I'm not finished when he gets here.'

'Certainly. Isn't that what I do best?' The smirk said it all.

'How dare you march into my business, intimidate my assistant, and make yourself at home.' I snarled, stepping around to the other side of my desk. 'And get your feet off the furniture.' The monster was reclining on one of the expensive leather sofas with his dirty shoes on the Tasmanian Oak coffee table.

He stood up. 'Mr Culley does not appreciate being ignored. I'm to take you to him immediately.'

'Well, that's not going to happen. I have a full diary this morning. I'm seeing clients. Tell him I'll come by later this afternoon. If I get time.'

I watched the face twist in confusion. This was a new thing for him and for me. I never ignored my father, and this accessory wasn't used to being argued with.

'You'll come now. That's what he has ordered.'

'Look. We can stand here and argue all day,' I said. 'I'm not going with you. And if you force me, my very observant assistant will call my friend the police detective. Off you go.'

An uneasy silence filled the void left by the accessory. Ferdinand showed my client into my office.

———

I answered the seventeen-hundredth call my father made with "What?" Ignoring my business for days on end had to stop. Today it did. But I was tired, grumpy, and hungry. And horny. All I could think about was getting back to Ebony.

'This day will not repeat,' my father said.

'In what way?' I asked, feigning stupidity.

'You will not ignore me ever again. You will answer my fucking calls. You will come to my office when I say so.'

'Actually, I won't. Get used to what happened today because that is the future. I have a business to run, I am in a new relationship, and I have a life that doesn't include you.'

Dead silence. Well, wishful thinking. I knew he wasn't dead.

'May I ask a favour,' my father said, acerbic as ever.

I didn't answer. The question was rhetorical. He would ask for as many *favours* as he wanted and, short of hanging up on him, which ran through my mind, I would listen.

'Please return to Miss Makepeace's apartment and tear the place apart, looking for the remaining notebooks. It is imperative that I have them. Imperative. A matter of life and death.'

'Whose life and death?' I asked, not expecting a reply.

'I need to have them before her friend packs up all

Miss Makepeace's things to ready the apartment for sale.'

'I'll look one last time. But if I cannot find them, you will not badger me about them again. Understood?'

He didn't answer me–I can do rhetorical questions too.

'Find them,' he snarled. 'And I think your life is in danger. Be careful.' He hung up.

———

I found a car park in the street, which was rare, and decided to leave the SUV outside. I would only be home long enough to shower and change. Ebony sent a text saying she would prepare dinner. So much I didn't know about her, least of all could she cook more than one vegetarian dish.

I didn't need to turn the key in the lock. The door was ajar. I don't know which emotions pushed their way into my psyche first: anger, fear, dread, anxiety, or just plain hatred. He'd obviously sent one or more of his accessories to ransack my house looking for Ebony's notebooks. The bastard. *I'm going to kill him one of these days.*

Was he watching on the cameras he'd hidden through the townhouse? I assumed he was and took a very, very deep breath before stepping inside. I took acting lessons when I was a kid. Sometimes they paid off. This was one of those times. On this occasion, my character would be a calm idiot, who did not know the seriousness of his situation. I talked to myself about how the interior designer wasn't as good as my friend said she was, and how disappointed I was that I would have to clean up the mess.

'I'll be late for dinner,' I said to whoever was watching me. 'Oh. No, I won't. I don't have to do this now. It will still be here tomorrow, as Mum used to say.' I could feel him bristle.

I left the mess, went upstairs, took a quick shower, changed, and bounded out the front door. I locked it behind me. I couldn't wait to see Ebony, but told myself I should start calling her Sherryn in case I slipped up at some point.

23

SANDERSON (SANDY)

Detective Tomy started a search on her computer for company directors, for interested parties, for staff lists of Sapphire Publishing. She was looking for Sophie Marris. The company's web page showed photos of staff members, but curiously not a picture of Douglas Culley. Sophie Marris was there. She was one of the editors. Her bio said she had been with the company for five years, was a skilled editor, and enjoyed working with "her" authors.

'Okay. Now to search for her.'

'Talking to yourself again.' Sandy moved behind Tomy to see her computer screen.

'I could come back with the stock reply of it's the only way to have an intelligent conversation, but what's the point.'

'None,' Sandy said, pulling up a chair. 'What have you found?'

Tomy showed him Sapphire Publishing's web page and clicked on Sophie Marris's photo so he could read the bio.

'Nothing outstanding,' he said.

'I'm searching for her now. See if I can find an address.'

Tomy discovered Sophie's Facebook page, her Instagram account, and her LinkedIn profile. None of which shed a light on where she might live.

'Have to do it the hard way,' she said. 'You know, the way detectives used to go about finding people.'

'Yeah. The long way.' Sandy pulled a sad face and went over to his desk. 'I'll leave you to it.'

'Go through the police database to see if her name comes up anywhere,' Tomy said. 'I'll check VicRoads.'

Between them it took about four minutes to find Sophie Marris's name on the records. She had a drivers' licence, a car registered in her name, and she'd reported being stalked by someone unknown to her six months earlier.

'Let's pay her a visit,' Sandy said.

———

Sophie Marris lived in a suburb west of Melbourne. It was one of those suburbs a land developer had invented, so had no genuine soul. Not like the old towns around it that had sprung up as stop overs for travellers on the way to the goldfields in the 1850s. Still, the area was pleasant. The trees were well established, the houses were on big blocks, and there was infrastructure — schools, public transport, shops.

'I've only driven past this on the way to Ballarat or Bendigo,' Sandy said as Tomy told him to turn left at the next corner.

'I don't come this way at all, even to go to Ballarat. Never sighted the place. It looks as if it's been here for a long time, though.'

They parked the car in front of what looked to be a recently renovated double fronted brick house. The outside walls were rendered, the roof either expertly cleaned or replaced, and the garden was updated.

'Nice place,' Tomy said. 'In a good little pocket.'

'Thinking of buying here?' Sandy asked.

'I might look at it if I miss out on Miss Makepeace's flat in North Melbourne.'

They walked up the front path to the door, and Sandy pressed the button for the doorbell. They waited. No response. The dog next door barked itself into a stupor every time Sandy rang the doorbell, but no noise came from inside the house.

'You stay here and keep trying,' Tomy said. 'I'll see if the neighbours know where she is.'

Tomy knocked on the door of the house that had the barking dog. An older woman who looked as if she'd just gotten out of bed, opened it. Her hair stuck up in peaks, her face was red on one side, and she held a dressing gown tightly around her middle.

'She left about four weeks ago,' the woman said. 'Asked me to look after her cat. Bit annoying really, it's an indoor only cat and when the dog comes in, I have to keep them apart. Bloody cat is nasty to the dog.'

Tomy didn't engage in the conversation about the cat and dog. 'Do you know where she went, or how long she will be away?'

'Who wants to know?'

Tomy flashed her badge.

'She said she needed a break and would call me to let me know what's going on. She hasn't. She gave me money for cat food and said to text her if the cat needed to go to the vet. I haven't heard from her. You're the second lot of folks come looking for her.'

Tomy straightened up. 'Who else has been looking for her?'

'A couple of shady characters that I thought only existed in the movies. Dressed the same. Same size. Same height. Could be twins, but one was really ugly, and the other was cute.'

Tomy passed her business card to the woman. 'Please let me know if you hear from Sophie, or if those shady characters come back.'

'Sure thing.' The door closed as Tomy walked back to Sandy.

'The plot thickens,' Sandy said as Tomy drove them out of the invented suburb and back onto the Calder Freeway.

'And I think my suspicions of Douglas Culley are warranted. As far as I'm concerned, he is the prime suspect.'

Sandy wriggled in his seat. He would not sabotage Tomy's investigation if it led to charging Culley. Culley did not kill Ebony, but Sandy's stomach jumped into his throat when he thought about Brad protecting her. Culley would find a way to kill Ebony if he knew Brad had saved her. But why? And why was Sophie Marris missing?

'I think Ms Marris's disappearance has something to do with Sapphire Publishing,' Sandy said as Tomy sped up to pass a concrete mixer.

'I agree. Him wanting Ebony's notebooks is all connected somehow, too. We have to work this out.'

24

———

EBONY

Ebony watched Brad drive away. He left early, had to go back to his townhouse to clean up the mess left by his father's goons. He made her feel good, needed, wanted, but the arrangement would not work for her long term. She had to find somewhere else to go.

She opened her new laptop, logged in, and made breakfast while it fired up. Sipping coffee and munching on Vegemite toast at the kitchen bench, she typed in the address for one of the online real estate websites. It was killing her that her apartment was being sold; she had loved living in North Melbourne.

She stared off across the bench, through the French doors to the immaculate alfresco area, imagining Gabrielle's and James's faces, smiling, waving to her.

In the search area of the website, she clicked on "rent". From the options, she chose Warrnambool. Not wanting to leave Victoria, and certainly not planning on going north, Ebony had researched Warrnambool when Brad wasn't around. It was a large coastal town that had a great beach. It was a mecca for tourists in the summer, but Ebony could live with that. Tourists brought vibrancy to sleepy communities.

Oh my goodness, I had no idea how expensive renting is.

Ebony scrolled through the thirty-six offerings, some so dilapidated it was an insult to list them, others in reasonable condition, but the rent being asked was outrageous. She found a unit for $400 a week. It had two bedrooms, one bathroom, a large living space, a new kitchen, close to town and its services. It looked okay in the photos. She sent the agent an email. The logistics of getting there eluded her; she would worry about that if she heard from the agent.

She closed the laptop lid, put on a tracksuit, and set out for a walk along the foreshore. The sea air cleared her head and helped her think. Moving away, far away, was the only solution. Brad would get over her. Would she get over him? Too bad. She had to. His father's ominous presence hung over Brad and exhausted her.

She was gone for over an hour, and her phone, although it was in her pocket, was off. Turning it on when she got inside, she was bombarded by message and missed call tones. Detective Sanderson was trying to reach her. How did he get her number? Brad was the only one who had this number. She called Brad. No answer. Standing with the phone in her hand, she almost dropped it when it rang.

'Yes?'

'Meet me in Café Zerko in half an hour.'

Ebony didn't have time to question Sanderson. He hung up as soon as he had finished speaking. Hands shaking, she was even more resolute that she had to get out of Melbourne. She showered, dressed, put on a hat and sunglasses, and walked the back way to the café strip on Pier Street.

Café Zerko was the one she had ruled out on her search for a quiet place a couple of weeks ago. She opened the door and saw Sandy sitting in the back. He didn't summon her over, but she told the waiter she was meeting someone and headed for the table. Sitting down, she took off her hat, but left the sunglasses on.

'Well?' she said.

'I can't find Brad.' Sandy's voice quivered, and he looked as if he had been crying.

'What? He was at my place last night. He left about six this morning. He was going home to clean up the mess his father's goons made of his townhouse.'

'I know.'

'How do you know?' Ebony looked around, suddenly on edge. She had a sinking feeling that Sandy had led Douglas Culley to her. But she couldn't see anyone who didn't fit in.

'Brad tells me everything. He didn't tell me where you were, but it didn't take much to figure it out.'

Ebony opened her mouth to speak then paused before saying, 'You, Brad, and I, are the only ones who know the truth. They're not here.'

'Who's not here?'

'Culley and his gang.'

Ebony put her hands on the table, folding and unfolding them. 'What is going on?'

Sandy leaned in a little closer. 'Brad asked me to help him clean up. The mess was extensive. I got to his place around six-thirty this morning. I waited until seven and then started calling to find out where he was. He didn't respond. He still hasn't responded. His car isn't in the street. I don't know if it's in the garage. I called his office and spoke to Ferdinand.'

Ebony turned her head slightly.

'He is Brad's personal assistant. He said he hadn't seen Brad since he left the office yesterday afternoon. This is not like him. He tells me everything. His father has been harassing him about your notebooks. He is harassing me, too. Even got your mother to call me for an added harassment level.'

'Oh, my poor mother,' Ebony sighed. 'She does not know who she is dealing with.'

'And it won't matter. She will be in the dark. She is safe. Your contact at the publishers was an editor, Sophie Marris?'

'Yes. She was the only one I dealt with. When I saw Culley at my funeral, telling my mother he was my publisher I was bewildered. I knew Sophie didn't own the company, but she never mentioned a boss, never mentioned Culley. He isn't even on their website.'

'I know. Tomy and I are looking for Sophie. She is missing. We think she is safe. It appears she took off on her own accord. She left her cat with a neighbour. Something scared her.'

'I feel sick.' Ebony pulled a tissue out of her pocket and wiped her eyes. 'Now what?'

'We'll order coffee. It's rude to sit in a café and not order something. Then you will walk back to your house as if everything is fine, and I will drive to work. I'll text you the next step.'

———

Ebony called Brad. There was no answer. She didn't leave a message. All she wanted to do was throw her few belongings into a bag and leave. But she was feeling safe knowing that Culley didn't know she was here. She would wait until she heard from Sandy.

The laptop sat on the kitchen bench where she'd left it. She opened the lid and the tell-tale beep of an email sounded. It was from the agent in Warrnambool. Could she look at the unit? *Shit.*

Framing a pleasant reply, she read it twice before hitting send:

Thank you for getting back to me so quickly. Sadly, something has come up and I am not in a position to act just yet. I am still interested, so keep me in mind, and I will let you know when I'm ready to move. Thank you. Sherryn Forbes.

She almost signed Ebony Makepeace, but was forcing herself to remember that Ebony was dead.

Ebony went upstairs to make her bed. The t-shirt Brad slept in was on the pillow on his side. She picked it up; it smelt like him, like his expensive cologne. She folded it up and put it under the pillow *for next time,* she told herself.

She moved to the balcony and started looking through her notebooks while waiting for Sandy to text. In book number four, about a third of the way in, Ebony froze. Her eyes scanned the text, her head started pounding in time with her heartbeat. She wiped her hands on her pants to clear the sweat. She read the words to herself, afraid that if she said them aloud, they would develop a life of their own.

The next book I'm going to tackle will focus on corporate greed. I won't base it on a real business, but one I make up (can't be too careful, don't want to be sued). The company will be primarily a mining one – gold – but the CEO will also have his fingers in lots of other pies. The CEO is a ruthless tyrant who manipulates his two sons and does everything he can to get his own way. The mining company is being charged for irregularities under the Environment Protection Act. One of his sons is giving evidence for the Environmental Protection Agency. The tyrant has this son killed. His wife has disappeared, the sons don't know where she is, they've been told she is dead.

Ebony ran to the ensuite and vomited up the Vegemite toast and the coffee. She sat on the floor.

'Oh, my God. Oh my God. Oh my God. How could I have forgotten I wrote this? This was all in the first draft I sent to Sophie. This is what she wanted to talk to me about. I wonder if Culley read the draft. Of course he did. Why else would he want me dead. Why else would he want my notebooks?' Ebony squeezed her eyes shut and rocked back and forth.

Her phone buzzed. It was on the bedside table where she'd left it when she made the bed. She couldn't stand up. Her legs shook, her head spun and her stomach heaved like she'd just gotten off a roller coaster. She sat on the ensuite floor taking deep breaths, telling herself she was Sherryn Forbes. Ebony was dead. Culley couldn't find her.

The deep breaths helped to calm her a little, but she still couldn't stand up. She crawled over to the bed and pulled herself up to sit on it. She picked up the phone. Sandy had called and messaged. As she was about to read the message, he called again.

'Hello,' Ebony said in a whisper.

'It's Sandy,' he grumbled into the phone. 'Can you make your way into our office in the city? Tomy needs to be filled in on what's happened, and that Brad is missing.'

Ebony breathed slowly. It was barely audible.

'Ae you there?'

'Yes. I'm not well. I'm sick. Can it wait a while?'

'No, it can't. Brad is missing. Doesn't that bother you?'

'Of course it bothers me,' she snapped. 'It will take me a while. I have to clean up. Text me the address.' She hung up and made her way back to the ensuite. *Maybe a shower will help.*

———

Ebony put her sunglasses on, paid the taxi driver, put her bag over her shoulder, and stepped onto the curb. The police building occupied half the block and ominously stretched above the older buildings surrounding it. She texted Sandy that she was here, and lent up against the wall outside waiting for him to collect her. The sides of the building created a wind tunnel, so Ebony moved closer to the door. She didn't want to go in and face the police officers at the front desk by herself. She wanted Sandy to escort her through. Unhindered.

'This way, Ebony,' Sandy said when he saw her.

'She moved in close to him. 'No. Do not call me that in public. I am Sherryn Forbes.'

'Oh. Okay. Good point. Do you have any ID?'

'Yes.'

'Get it out. The officers on security will record your details and give you a pass before we go upstairs.'

Ebony pulled Sherryn Forbes's driver's licence out of her wallet and forced a smile as she showed it to the officer. He wrote her details in the visitor's book. He didn't speak or look at her when he handed her a visitor's pass.

'Happy chap,' Ebony said as Sandy pushed the button to call the elevator.

'He's probably been there all night,' Sandy said. 'Let me do the talking with Tomy. Only speak when she asks you something. Okay?'

Ebony nodded. Her stomach rolled as the elevator stopped on the nominated floor. She followed Sandy, willing herself not to be sick, taking deep breaths.

Sandy walked up to Tomy's desk and lent in to speak to her.

The woman looked at her partner and frowned. 'Can't it wait?' she said. 'I'm still looking for Sophie.'

Ebony put her hand over her mouth and looked around frantically for the bathroom. She wasn't going to make it. Seeing a small rubbish bin on the floor next to someone else's desk, she picked it up, turned her back to as many people as she could, and brought up the rest of her breakfast.

'Nice,' Tomy said. 'Friend of yours? Bathroom's over there, miss,' Tomy snarled. Ebony saw the meanness dripping from the corner of her mouth.

'Thanks.' Ebony took the rubbish bin and made her way to the bathroom. She cleaned the bin under the tap in a washbasin, splashed water on her face, and rinsed her mouth. The woman in the mirror was fragile, afraid, and vulnerable. Ebony didn't recognise her. With the cleaned bin in hand, she went back to Tomy's desk.

'Are you okay?' Sandy asked.

Ebony nodded and put the bin on the floor where she'd found it.

'Let's go into the meeting room,' Sandy suggested.

Still frowning and oozing venom, Tomy walked ahead, opened the door of the room, and found herself a seat. 'What's going on? I'm busy.'

Sandy showed Ebony to a seat on the other side of the table, put a clean bin next to her, and sat down a seat away.

'I have a lot to say,' Sandy began, looking directly at Tomy. 'Only interrupt if you want clarification on a point. Do not yell or make unseemly noises. We'll both lose our jobs and be in a shitload of trouble if you do. Clear?'

Tomy nodded. A reluctant, petulant, self-absorbed nod. Ebony could still see the venom.

'This young lady sitting next to me was signed in downstairs as Sherryn Forbes. She is, in fact, Ebony Makepeace.'

Tomy stood up. 'I don't have time for games, for your antics or your crap.'

'Sit down, Tomy. Please. Listen.'

She sat down with a thump and banged her fists on the table.

Ebony jumped.

'My best friend is Bradley Culley.' Sandy stopped speaking to look at Tomy's reaction. Her eyes widened and her mouth tightened into an angry line. 'He was ordered by his father to kill Miss Makepeace here. He didn't know why, just that she was a problem to be dealt with.'

Tomy put up her hand. 'Why was Brad tasked with this? Is he an assassin? Is that his job? Nice friends you have.'

'No, Tomy, he isn't. And as you can see by Miss Makepeace's presence, he didn't do it. But he knew she had to die to appease his father. So he asked for my help, and I found a Jane Doe who had been on ice for a few weeks, who had an uncanny resemblance to our murder victim. They buried her in Miss Makepeace's place and Brad organised a new identity for our writer here.' Sandy stopped to give Tomy a chance to absorb the information.

'Go on.'

Ebony noticed Tomy's gaze was not quite as vicious.

'Ebony went to her own funeral and heard her mother speaking to Douglas Culley. She didn't know Culley owned Sapphire Publishing. She had only ever dealt with her editor, Sophie Marris. Ebony heard Culley ask her mother for her notebooks.'

'I'm listening,' Tomy said.

'You and I know as well as Ebony that Culley is obsessed with getting her notebooks, but we still don't know why.'

'I do,' Ebony said, her voice hoarse from vomiting.

Both detectives glared at her.

Ebony got notebook number four out of her bag and put it on the table. 'I've marked the beginning page with a Post-it-Note.'

Tomy grabbed the book and turned to the page. 'I don't understand,' she murmured. 'Fill me in, Miss... whoever you are.' Tomy passed the book to Sandy.

'The draft I sent to Sophie was the book based on these notes. When I saw a connection, I researched Culley's business. It's as if my draft is a timeline of company events. Brad's brother has disappeared. Brad is now missing. I heard you say you were looking for

Sophie, and Culley's company is under investigation for environmental vandalism. His son Steven instigated the proceedings and was a witness for the prosecution.'

Ebony's revelations were news to Sandy as much as Tomy. The detectives looked at each other. Ebony could almost see their brains processing the data, putting all the pieces of the puzzle into their appropriate places.

'I'm furious with you, Sandy. The time I wasted looking for Ebony's killer. That in itself is a crime, let alone faking a murder. She will have to stay as Sherryn Forbes. Ebony Makepeace is indeed dead. I'm not losing my job over some botched assassination.

Sandy patted Ebony on the knee. 'Are you all right?'

'Not really. Brad is missing, Sophie is missing. God knows what happened to Brad's mother, and where is his brother? And Douglas Culley is untouchable.'

'No. He's not,' Tomy growled. 'We're going to pay him a visit. You go home, Miss Forbes. Sandy and I will pay Culley a visit. May we keep this notebook?'

Ebony nodded and picked up her bag. She moved the bin near the door where it had lived before she came into the room.

'Thanks for all the information,' Tomy said as Ebony took her leave.

'You're welcome. Let's hope you can solve this.' Ebony closed the door behind her, relieved Tomy had softened.

25

SANDERSON (SANDY)

Tomy waited until Ebony was out of the door and out of earshot before turning on Sandy. 'How many laws have you broken? How many?' She was right in his face. Spittle spewed from her mouth.

Sandy backed away, the spittle shower not to his liking. 'Not many, I don't think. There was no murder committed.'

'What about the waste of resources and Department time, mine especially?' She slumped down onto a chair. 'Tell me what else is going on.'

'Brad is missing. I was to meet him at his place this morning at six thirty. He didn't show. Not like him, he is always early, an annoying habit.'

'Get on with it.' Tomy's patience seemed to evaporate with the ticking of the clock on the wall.

'I waited until seven before calling him.'

'Why were you meeting him so early?'

'Someone trashed his place the day before. He got home from work and found it, then went to Ebony's. He was going to clean up this morning, with my help.'

'Who trashed it? And don't say you don't know, because I KNOW YOU DO,' Tomy roared into Sandy's face.

'On the phone, he said it could only be the goons who worked for his father. They would have been looking for the notebooks. His father had pressured, threatened, and bullied him into finding them.'

'She had them all along?'

'No. Once she was dead she couldn't go back to the apartment. I got them out for her and gave them to Brad.'

'Sneaky bastard,' Tomy mumbled. 'Something else you hid from me.'

'You know what?' Sandy levelled. 'I was trying to keep you safe. You not knowing meant you couldn't go off half-cocked and get yourself into trouble.'

'Like we are going to do now?' she asked.

'Yes. Like we are going to do now. You drive.'

———

Tomy and Sandy flashed their badges at the goon waiting for them outside the elevator on the third floor.

'Mr Culley isn't here,' the goon said before being asked.

'Yes, he is,' Tomy snapped, pushing past the man who was twice her size.

Sandy followed.

'Detectives,' Culley greeted when they walked into the office foyer. 'What can I do for you?'

'You'll find us a seat in your office. We will all sit down and have a civilised chat,' Sandy said, surprised by his own bravado.

'Certainly, come in. But I can only spare you a few

minutes. I am seeing someone who made an appointment.'

'Sarcasm sits well with you,' Tomy mocked. 'Where is Sophie Marris, and where is your son, Bradley?'

'And,' Sandy interjected, 'we want to see the death certificates of your wife and your eldest son, Steven.'

Culley's expression did not change. His disconcerting stare fell on each in turn. 'I don't know what you are talking about. Ms Marris sent a resignation email. Very rude. I won't provide the death certificates without a warrant. And I do not know where Junior is.'

'Who is Junior?' Tomy asked.

'That's what I call my youngest son. The annoying, trite, belligerent bastard that he is.'

'Okay,' Tomy continued. 'When was the last time you saw Bradley?'

'A few days ago, but I spoke to him on the phone the day before yesterday. He refused to follow my instructions. Again.'

'What instructions?'

'That's not your business, Detective.'

'We think it is,' Sandy said.

'Just because you are a friend of his doesn't mean you have the right to know about the conversations between Junior and me.'

Sandy flinched. Brad's father remembered him.

'There's more to this, and we are very close to completing the puzzle,' Sandy said, staring into those grey, unfeeling eyes.

'What puzzle? What are you talking about?'

'Who trashed Brad's place yesterday? Why was Sophie Marris trying to contact Miss Makepeace a couple of days before Miss Makepeace was shot? Why did Sophie leave her house abruptly, dumping her cat on her neighbour? Why were you hassling Brad for Miss Makepeace's notebooks?'

At this last question, Culley moved in his seat, his lips pursed, and a cloud of hatred veiled his face.

Sandy continued, 'And why did you have Mrs Makepeace ring and nag me for Ebony's notebooks after I told you the police department didn't have them?'

'Because I knew you were lying. My men saw you go to Miss Makepeace's apartment and come out with more than you took in. Now get out. I have an appointment.' Culley stood and folded his arms over his ample middle.

'A couple more questions, Mr Culley,' Tomy said. 'We won't keep you long.'

Culley kept standing.

'How did Sophie Marris work out that Ebony Makepeace's draft contained a blow by blow description of what is happening to your mining company? Did she put two and two together and confront you about the pollution and Steven's disappearance, or did you monitor her emails and phone? Simple questions.' Tomy stood and folder her arms across her middle, which was not so ample.

'I am not answering any more of your questions,' Culley said, his face looking as flushed as someone about to have a heart attack.

'Of course you're not. We will wait until we arrest you and question you at the office.'

'Arrest me for what? You're chasing up the wrong tree, detective. You are picking on the wrong person.'

'Glad to see you are so upset about Brad being missing,' Sandy said as he and Tomy left.

26

EBONY

Ebony was exhausted. She opened the door of the Altona house, locked it behind her, threw the keys onto the hall table, and took off her shoes. She made her way into the bright, airy kitchen that usually filled her with peace, but today left her feeling empty and even more alone.

She tried Brad's number again. Still no answer.

She made a cup of tea and took it upstairs to sit on the balcony to read notebook five. The wind had turned and was coming from the south, bringing with it a biting cold. She closed the French doors and sat on the couch. It faced the windows, but the view wasn't as clear.

Notebook five, the one she was working on when Brad shot her—she instinctively reached to her left side—hadn't been written in since. She started on page one. Her notes planned a sequel to the book she had drafted in notebook four, the book Sophie had tried to speak to her about. In the sequel the CEO got his just desserts and good prevailed over evil, but she hadn't put any meat on the bones, it was all sketchy and flaky. She'd been side-tracked by another project she had moved on to. Culley wouldn't have found anything interesting in this notebook.

The nausea that plagued Ebony in the morning came back with a vengeance and she ran for the bathroom. She hadn't eaten since breakfast, so the effort of dry retching only brought up bile. She felt awful. Was this fear nagging at her very being? If so, she had to get away. But could she leave knowing Brad was missing? *Is he dead?* She burst into tears. This was all too much. She wished she could be like the female protagonists in her novels.

She pushed herself away from the toilet bowl and had another shower. Sandy called four times while she was drowning in a sea of water droplets.

She called him back.

'Miss Forbes. We have made a start,' he said in a matter-of-fact tone. 'We have ruffled feathers. Stay home. I will be in touch tomorrow.'

Ebony didn't respond. There was no need. She hung up and climbed into bed.

As promised, Sandy called early the next morning. 'Did you sleep okay?' he asked when Ebony answered the phone.

'No.'

'Me either.'

'Can you come into the office this morning? Around 10?'

'Sure.' Ebony looked in the mirror and decided another shower was in order. She wondered who would pay the bills, especially the water bill, if they didn't find Brad.

———

'Thanks for coming in again,' Tomy said, indicating which chair Ebony should sit on. 'We've upset Douglas Culley, and are waiting for him to make a mistake.'

Tomy told Ebony about the meeting the day before.

'So you think he has done something to Brad?' Ebony almost suffocated as she tried to hold back the grief.

'Yes. And Sophie. But we're hoping Sophie got away before he cornered her.'

'Why would he do anything to Brad? Brad did everything he asked.' Ebony's face contorted trying to stifle the hatred she felt for Culley.

'Brad didn't do everything. As far as we know, Culley still thinks you are dead, but he pressured Brad relentlessly into finding your notebooks. We think he has perhaps kidnapped Brad to get the information out of him.' Sandy swallowed and wiped his face with a handkerchief.

'What are you going to do now?' Ebony asked.

Tomy leaned over the table and stared at Ebony.

'We are going to make sure he fucks up so we can arrest him. We're going back to his office. You should wait here. Our colleagues will show you where the cafeteria is,' Tomy said as she and Sandy left the room.

27

SANDERSON (SANDY)

The detectives expected resistance to their unannounced visit, but there was none. The goon at the entrance let them in without complaint, and Culley ushered them into his office, where his solicitor sat, the smuggest of looks on his well-to-do face.

'This is my solicitor,' Culley said without offering Sandy or Tomy a seat.

Tomy walked into the foyer and pulled a chair from the waiting area, dragging it into Culley's office. Sandy copied.

'That's better,' Tomy said, crossing her legs. 'Let's get started.'

'Mr Solicitor,' Sandy said, looking at the perfectly coiffured man. 'No need to introduce yourself. We'll get to know each other quite well in due course, I imagine. Anyway, my colleague and I have credible information that your client was involved in the murder of Miss Ebony Makepeace, the disappearance of Sophie Marris and the disappearance of Bradley Culley. We also suspect he's involved in the deaths or disappearances of his wife and his eldest son.' Sandy wiped his hands on his trousers.

'Prove it,' the solicitor said.

'Oh, we will. Don't worry,' Tomy quipped. 'Bear with me while I fill you in. Miss Makepeace sent the draft of her latest novel to her editor at Sapphire Publishing, Sophie Marris. Miss Marris read the draft and realised it was very close to the reality of the situation Mr Culley's mining business was embroiled in, including the disappearance of his eldest son, who was going to give evidence for the prosecution. This "coincidence" sent alarm bells ringing and Miss Marris tried to contact Miss Makepeace to talk about the similarities. But, Miss Makepeace was shot, and later died, so Miss Marris did not get to speak to her. Somehow Miss Marris became aware that Culley knew about the book. Fearing for her life, she quickly organised an escape, leaving her cat with a neighbour. Poor cat. Do you follow so far?' Tomy looked at the solicitor.

'I'll go on. We don't know if Miss Marris successfully escaped to safety, or if your client here did away with her like he did Miss Makepeace.'

The solicitor lent forward and was about to speak, but Tomy put up her hand to shush him. 'That brings us to Bradley. His home was ransacked the day before he disappeared. Coincidentally at a time in his relationship with his father, where he refused to be bullied any longer and was not going to search for Miss Makepeace's notebooks. By the way, we have them. The notebooks. That's how we worked out what you'd done, Culley.' Tomy folded her arms across her middle.

'What do you mean, worked it out?' Culley roared.

'One of Ebony's notebooks has the plan for the story she sent to Sophie. You had the draft of the novel, but you also needed the notebook where it was all planned. Our IT Department got into the laptop, and we had access to all her emails. You'd be surprised to know that we found the draft she sent to Sophie in her "sent" folder. That one slipped by you.'

Finished with her recount, Tomy stood up and paced around the room, waiting for Culley to respond.

Culley's grey eyes darted from Tomy and Sandy to his solicitor.

'Don't speak,' the solicitor said to Culley. 'Good day, detectives. You have circumstantial evidence that is not enough to charge my client.'

With grins on their faces as wide as the clown at the entrance to Luna Park, Tomy and Sandy left.

'We have him,' Tomy said when they got into the car.

'All we have to do is find the proof. His solicitor was right, it is circumstantial.' Sandy put on his sunglasses as Tomy pulled into the traffic.

———

The number for the incoming call on Tomy's phone was unknown to her, but she answered politely. It was Miss Marris's neighbour.

'You told me to call you if anything happened,' she said. 'Two men who looked like twins broke into her house this morning.'

'Did you call the police?' Tomy asked.

'Aren't you the police?'

'Yes, but if you'd called triple zero, a car might have arrived while they were still there.'

'They are still there. They've been there for a couple of hours. Do you want me to dial triple zero?'

'YES,' Tomy yelled into the phone. 'I'll be there as soon as possible.'

She filled Sandy in on the way.

Sophie Marris's neighbour greeted the detectives when they pulled up out front.

'They left. The crooks, before the cops got here.'

'What did the police officers say to you?' Sandy asked, before he and Tomy went into the house to speak to their uniformed colleagues.

'Wanted to know where the owner was, and would I know if anything was taken. I wouldn't unless it was clear a TV was once in a space or something.'

'Thank you for letting me know,' Tomy said, pulling Sandy's arm.

With their IDs ready, the detectives walked through the front door. If the neighbour had not seen Culley's goons break in, they wouldn't have known anyone had been there.

'Not like Brad's place,' Sandy mumbled.

'Apart from the broken lock on the front door, there's no evidence of anything being disturbed,' a uniformed officer said. 'Do you know how to contact the owner?'

Sandy sighed the sigh of frustration and anger. 'No. We are looking for her in relation to a case we're working on.'

'Let us know if you find her,' the officer said handing Sandy his card. He gave him his.

'We have to go back to see Culley, don't we?' Sandy asked as he slid behind the steering wheel. 'I'm driving. You drive like a lunatic when you are obsessed with something.'

———

The bodyguards stood next to each other to block the door.

'You left Miss Marris's place quite tidy, didn't you? If the neighbour hadn't seen you break in, no one would know you were there. What were you looking for? Doesn't matter, we'll ask your boss. Get out of the way, or we'll arrest you now. You've heard of a thing called DNA, I guess. Fingerprints are so last century.' Sandy took a step forward.

The men separated to let he and Tomy pass.

'What, no solicitor, this time?' Tomy jibed at Culley.

Both detectives watched as their suspect's face went from an angry red to an even angrier purple.

'What do you want now?' he snarled.

Tomy started reciting Culley's rights as she moved around the desk to arrest him.

The sound of gunfire suddenly filled the air and Tomy collapsed to the ground. Sandy pulled his weapon and fired at Culley. The man dropped like a lead balloon.

For a moment, Sandy froze. His heart stopped; his mind numbed. The goons running in brought him back to reality, and he leapt behind the desk to see to Tomy. She had a horrific wound on the right side of her abdomen. Blood oozed out relentlessly. He called triple zero, trying to keep the panic in his voice subdued, so he made sense to the operator, then pushed his sergeant's number in his contacts. '

Tomy is down. Shot by Culley.'

———

Ebony sat next to Sandy at Tomy's bedside.

'Thank goodness she is going to make it,' she said.

Sandy nodded. 'All we have to do is find Brad, then the case will be closed. The goons are in custody. I'll question them later. At the moment, we can hold them for breaking and entering.'

'What about Sophie?' Ebony asked.

'She called yesterday. Saw on the news that Culley was dead. She's going home. She'll come in to see me in a day or so.'

'Will you tell her about me?'

'No. Ebony Makepeace is dead. We have to pin something on that arsehole, Culley. What will you do?'

'I'll stay in in Altona, so you will know where to reach me when you find him.'

'And we will find him,' Sandy said, wiping his eyes. 'I miss him.'

'So do I.'

28

EBONY

Sandy knocked politely on Ebony's door. He waited for her to answer; she was expecting him.

'Come in,' the young woman said, letting him pass. 'What news?'

'We've been through Brad's townhouse four times. Collected DNA samples and matched some with the goons we knew were responsible, but all that does is prove they were there.'

Ebony put the kettle on while Sandy made himself comfortable on the couch. 'It's a lovely outlook here, isn't it?' he said staring through the French doors to the small garden outside.

'Yes. The landscapers Brad used did a great job.'

'Have you come to terms with your new identity?'

'Took longer without Brad here to help me along. But as you often reminded me, Ebony Makepeace is dead.'

She made tea and put Sandy's on the coffee table. 'It's been four weeks. We're not going to find Brad alive, are we?'

'One of the bodyguards talked. That's why I wanted to see you. He said they didn't kidnap Brad or

157

kill him. They were told to look for your notebooks at his townhouse, to make a big mess, to make a point. But they didn't go back the next morning. They didn't kidnap him.'

'Do you believe that?'

'Yes.'

'So what is your theory?' Ebony asked, sitting down on her favourite armchair, her feet tucked under her. 'Have you spoken to Sophie Marris?'

'My theory is that Douglas Culley used someone else—or even himself—to take Brad. Now Culley's dead, there's no way of asking him. Yes. Sophie is back in her home and starting a new job.' Sandy sipped his tea. 'Do you have any biscuits?'

———

Ebony got the taxi to stop a few doors down from Brad's place in South Melbourne. She hadn't been there since he disappeared; the police had been all over it. From where she stood, the townhouse looked like it had when Brad was in it. The police tape had gone, and someone had put his rubbish bins out.

She didn't have a front door key, but she had a remote for the garage and used it to get inside. His coal black SUV sat alone waiting patiently for its owner.

Even though he had been missing for five weeks, the house still smelt like him. Moving through the living room, she thought she heard something upstairs. She stood still and listened. There it was again; someone was walking around on the second level. If there were carpet throughout like there was in her place, she wouldn't have heard anything. Cupboards opened and closed, drawers banged shut, and furniture scraped along the floor. She cringed. Brad had spent a fortune having the floorboards sanded and repolished.

Heavy footsteps made their way to the top of the staircase. She hid behind the couch, the only place where she would be out of view from the stairs.

It annoyed Ebony that she couldn't see the man's face—the footsteps indicated a man —so she put her phone on silent and held it out alongside the couch and kept touching the button to take photos. Her heart pounded in her chest. She could hear it drumming in her ears and feel it pulsing behind her eyes. Terror. The same feeling she had the day Brad pulled the trigger in the café.

She waited while the man yanked out drawers and opened cupboards in the kitchen and laundry. The couch shielded her from his roving eyes and would do so unless he moved to look behind it. Reason told her he wouldn't. She was hiding in the gap between the couch and the window, her body stretched out to fit in the space.

Seemingly finished with his search, the man left the house through the front door. Ebony stayed on the floor until her heartbeat slowed to normal and she was certain he had gone. She crawled out from behind the couch, but sat on the floor under the window, her legs crossed, so she wasn't visible from outside.

Tapping the pictures icon, Ebony went through the photos. She'd taken six. The first three were useless, but the last three clearly showed the figure. She expanded the images and almost choked on her own breath. He looked so much like Brad, but it wasn't Brad. She zoomed in further on the last one; he had the same grey eyes as Brad's father. Ebony put her hand over her mouth to stifle the nausea. Then she called Sandy.

———

Ebony had invited Sandy and Tomy to dinner. She wanted to show them the photos calmly. Tomy was still recovering from the gunshot wound, and Sandy seemed quite fragile.

'Dinner won't be long.' Ebony poured her guests a drink.

'Smells good,' Tomy said, nodding in appreciation of the wine.

'Not sure if you know I'm vegetarian,' Ebony said. 'Don't be disappointed when you don't see an animal carcass on your plate.'

'Gee thanks, that's a lovely image,' Tomy grumbled. 'Ebony was vegetarian. I was hoping Sherryn Forbes wasn't.'

'Funny.' Ebony got out the plates.

'I'm sure it will be wonderful.' Sandy helped Tomy to the table. 'I appreciate anything I don't have to prepare myself.'

While her guests helped themselves to seconds, Ebony got her phone out of her pocket. She clicked the pictures icon and zoomed in on the photo that looked most like Brad, except for those eyes.

Sandy put his hand over his mouth to stop the food he was choking on, spurting onto the table. 'Oh my God,' he rasped. 'That's Steven. Brad's brother. Why was he at Brad's? We thought he was dead.'

Ebony felt sick. 'This gets worse by the day. He was clearly looking for something when he was stomping around Brad's.'

'This shines another light on things. Gonna have to chat with the goons again.' Sandy swallowed the last of the wine.

'Are they still in custody?' Ebony asked.

'Yep. Internal investigation into Culley's death and Tomy being shot. They were witnesses,' he said with a wry smile. 'And their DNA was found at Sophie Marris's place. We'd better go, Tomy.' Sandy helped his partner off her chair. 'I've got a busy day tomorrow.'

'Thank you for dinner, Ebony,' Tomy said. 'I have a better appreciation of what it is not to eat an animal carcass.' She grinned while reaching out to give Ebony a hug.

29

SANDERSON (SANDY)

Accessories One and Two were happy to chat when Sandy told them they would be able to go if they cooperated, and the only charge they would face was breaking and entering into Sophie Marris's house.

'Get a good lawyer and you have a Community Corrections Order,' Sandy said as the men sat in the chairs on the other side of the table in the interview room.

'Unusual to talk to us together, isn't it?' Accessory One said.

'I'm in a hurry and not in the mood for games. You can do a tag team if you want. I don't care. I just want information. We'll start with where is Bradley Culley.

The two men looked at each other, and Accessory Two nodded.

'We don't know for certain, but you need to know that Douglas Culley was not the one in charge,' Accessory One said.

Sandy didn't speak immediately. He hadn't expected this, and it needed time to go into his brain for processing. 'Go on. I'm listening.'

'Someone else pulled the strings. Mr Culley was

the puppet. And he had no idea whose orders he was following. The threats, whatever they were, kept him in check. To everyone, it looked like he ran the show, even company records, bank accounts. Everything pointed to Douglas Culley being in charge. Bradley was fooled too.'

'And you?' Sandy asked. 'You two seem quite intelligent today compared with the roles you played working for Culley.'

'We didn't work for Douglas Culley. We worked for the puppeteer.'

'Sandy made sure the recorder was working before he encouraged the two men to continue their story. 'And who is that?'

Accessory One looked around the room before he answered the question, as if he were checking to see if anyone else was there. 'Steven Culley.'

'But Brad told me Steven had disappeared, feared dead,' Sandy said.

'Douglas Culley ordered Brad to kill Steven. He wanted him out of the way. Steven had concocted some scenario that he was going to give evidence against Mr Culley's company in a pollution case against it—needed to boost his credentials for a big corporate raid or something. Mr Culley panicked.'

Sandy poured the men a fresh glass of water, and nodded for them to continue.

'Steven is a psychopath, but Brad couldn't kill his brother. He convinced their father that Steven was dead, but instead of killing him, set him up with a new identity. Steven wasn't going away quietly though, establishing his own alternate life, and manipulating his father from a distance. From Hell.

'When Steven found out about Miss Makepeace's

book—he was sleeping with Sophie Marris by the way—but she didn't know his real identity, he decided Ebony had to go. Brad was the ideal assassin: obedient, loyal, trustworthy. Mr Culley was given his orders and Brad stalked his victim. But just like he couldn't kill his brother, he couldn't kill Miss Makepeace.'

'Wait. What do you mean, he couldn't kill Miss Makepeace?'

'Seriously, detective. We are professional investigators among several other things. We picked up the signs. Brad did a good job until he moved Miss Makepeace into his house in Altona. But Douglas Culley thought she was dead. We told Steven she wasn't. He lost interest in her when her life fell apart and she had to run. But he wanted her notebooks and would do anything to get them.'

'I wondered about her being in Brad's place in Altona, but he was certain it was all fine.' Sandy shook his head and gulped water from his glass. 'Did Douglas Culley find out Steven was alive?'

Accessory Two continued the story. 'Steven marched into the office two days before you and your bossy partner confronted Mr Culley the first time. Steven stood in front of his father's desk, hands on hips, an evil smirk that spread over his whole face, and tormented him by not speaking for at least five minutes. We thought Mr Culley was going to have a heart attack.'

Sandy stood up and paced the room. 'And Douglas Culley's death?'

'Suicide by cop, we think. He was up against it. Nowhere to go.'

Sandy's heart sank. He'd shot the wrong villain, even though Culley shot Tomy first.

'Where is Steven Culley now?'

'He has a house in Torquay, a big house. We'll give you the address.'

'Thank you,' Sandy said, sincerity in his tone. 'Do you think Brad will be there?'

Both men nodded their heads.

'Go prepared for a battle,' Accessory One said.

'Please don't go too far away, in case I need to ask you more questions.' Sandy opened the door for the men, and watched their backs as they walked down the hallway. He knew he wouldn't see them again,

———

Sandy wanted to tell Ebony he had a lead on Brad's whereabouts, but this was a police matter; she would be the first one he called if he found Brad alive.

Tomy sat in the backseat. She wouldn't miss the wrapping up of this farcical case. She'd told Sandy as much when he filled her in.

Two cars drove down the Princes Freeway to Torquay. Sandy, Tomy, and another officer in one car, and the Sergeant and a police sniper in the other.

They didn't park in front of the house. Sandy, and the officer who sat in the passenger seat, got out and with guns drawn, used bushes and trees for cover, trying to get a look inside. The house was on one level and took up half the enormous block of land. A verandah hugged the house on every side. Sandy crept up on to the verandah and crawled along under the windows, listening. The other officer went around the back to do the same thing.

Sandy's phone vibrated; it was a text from his colleague saying he heard two male voices in what appeared to be the kitchen. Sandy crept along through an unkempt garden to the back. He heard two voices, Brad's he knew, the other he guessed was Steven's. He'd only met Steven once or twice.

Both detectives focussed on the voices. The fellow Sandy was with, had called their Sergeant who was listening in. But Sandy's brain had difficulty processing what his ears sent to it, and what he could see through a small pane of window glass.

'Before I hand you over to my assistants who will get you out of the way for good, I'll give you a parting gift.' Steven's voice filled the air with vitriol.

'What are you doing with that?' Brad yelled as Steven came toward him with a large fry pan in his hand.

'I'm going to break your ribs.' Steven's vindictive grin covered his face. 'I'm not going to hit your head because I want you conscious.'

Sandy watched Brad steel himself for the blow to his chest, but his attempts to stifle screams of agony were in vain. Steven slammed the heavy pan into Brad's ribs twice, then swung it at his arms and legs.

'You've been a great brother, Brad. But you've served your purpose. Thanks, bro. Ciao.'

'Steven. Steven. Untie me, you prick. Brad's voice trickled away with the increasing pain in his chest.

'You fucking bastard. I could have killed you when Father ordered it. I didn't.'

'Now, now, language. You remember what Mother used to say when we used foul language?'

'Where is Mother? Did you kill her? Tell me.'

'Ah, sadly, that's a secret for another day. I'll tell it to your Ebony Makepeace when I finish her off the way you should have. She saw me in your house the other day. I bet her curiosity is well and truly piqued. That surveillance system was worth the effort.'

Sandy decided not to wait any longer for the sniper or the Sergeant to get to the front of the house. He ran from the back and launched himself at Steven Culley before the man had closed the door behind him.

'Don't move. You're under arrest.'

30

BRAD

As soon as they released me from hospital, I hailed a taxi and gave the address on Esplanade Altona as my destination. There's nothing they can do for cracked ribs, apparently. I have to be brave and suffer the pain. Now that Steven is gone, that might be easier.

Ebony stood next to the letterbox, waiting for me. We would be face to face in freedom for the first time in our relationship. *Do we have a relationship, though?* We've had great sex, but she's dismissed me as quickly as she's jumped into bed with me. When the taxi pulled up, she opened the door for me, waited impatiently while I paid the driver, and helped me out.

'How are you feeling?' she asked needlessly. She knew how I was feeling. I called her as I was leaving the hospital.

'Same as when you asked me earlier,' I said, taking small steps toward the front door.

'I thought there might have been a miraculous turn around while you were in the taxi.'

'I wish.'

I shuffled my way to the open plan living/kitchen area and made my way to Ebony's favourite armchair.

'You may sit in it just this once,' she said.

'I'm teasing,' I said. 'I'd rather be on the couch in case I want to lie down.'

When I was in hospital Ebony had looked at the bruises on my abdomen and legs, which were healing, but the broken ribs were hindering my movement. It was difficult to breathe and walk at the same time.

'Sandy is calling by later. He wants to talk to you.'

'Of course he does. Can't leave a man in peace to make out with a wonderful woman.'

'What woman would that be? I'm not making out with you when you can't even breathe without pain.'

'But that's more painful. I'll be brave.' I winked at Ebony and asked her if I could have a cup of coffee. 'I haven't had a decent cup of coffee for weeks. Not since Steven kidnapped me. There's a machine in the pantry. Have you used it yet? You didn't use it for me before.' I pulled a sulky face hoping she would find it endearing.

It worked.

She made a coffee for each of us, putting two sugars in mine. 'I'll get you a tray to put on your lap, so you don't have to reach over to the coffee table,' she said.

'I'd rather have you on my lap.' I grinned and beckoned her toward me.

'I'm not going to be responsible for your broken ribs tearing a whole in your lungs,' she growled.

'If you are gentle, I'll be fine. Come over here.' I lay down on the couch stifling the groans that indicated pain.

Ebony moved her hands over my groin watching my willy grow. 'I'll help you with these dreadful tie up daggy pants will I?' she teased.

I moved my hips, so she had easier access while my willy developed a mind of its own. It had been a while.

I could tell Ebony was feeling the throbbing and warmth between her legs. She swayed a little when that happened. I moved to touch her.

'No. You lay still; I'll do all the work.' She watched the smile take over my face as she moved herself around on top of me.

When we were both ready—which hadn't taken very long—she spread her legs on either side of my body and lowered herself, being very careful not to touch my abdomen. As she moved herself up and down, we both groaned in appreciation of the other. It had indeed been a long time.

———

'You look happier with yourself than I thought you would.' Sandy reached out for my hand as he went to sit on the opposite couch.

I wanted to tell him that Ebony and I had just finished a good time before he arrived, but I thought that would be tacky. And there was lots I still didn't know about Ebony; it might annoy her if I shared what we'd been up to.

'We need to talk. I want your side of the story. The Sergeant says I have to tie up this messy case and you are the cause of most of the mess.'

I thanked Sandy for his consideration and his thoughtfulness. And challenged him to tell me what mess I'd made.

'You can't be serious?' he said with an exasperated sigh.

I loved his exasperated sighs.

'Tell me everything from when you left Ebony's that morning.'

I tried to sit up, but it was a losing battle. Sandy grabbed my hands and pulled me forward while I groaned like the beginnings of an earthquake. He moved my legs, so I was sitting on the couch instead of lying on it.

'Thanks, mate,' I said. 'It's an effort.'

'Comfortable?' he asked. 'Because if you are, get on with the story. I'm recording it. So behave.'

'Okay. I got home on the Tuesday night to find my place ransacked. A real effort was made to show me that someone had been inside without my permission, and had gone through my stuff. I couldn't be bothered with it and I'd arranged to go to Ebony's.'

Sandy stopped me.

'I suppose we can say her real name,' Sandy said, rubbing his forefinger across his chin. 'But we faked her death. If you call her Sherryn and Steven spills his guts, saying that you were supposed to kill Ebony but didn't, we are up shit creek without a paddle.'

'He won't say anything about ordering Ebony's death. He'll let our father take the blame for that. I'll say Sherryn.'

Sandy wiped the interview and we started again.

I repeated up to the point where I'd planned to go to Ebony's, changing her name to Sherryn.

'I got in the car and drove to my friend Sherryn's place at Altona. It's actually my place. She is staying there for a while.

I left at six the next morning and asked you to meet me at home at six thirty, to help me start the clean-up. There was no point making an official police complaint. I thought I knew who'd trashed my place—my father. Turns out it was my brother. Great family.'

'Go on,' Sandy niggled.

'I put the car in the garage. I'd toyed with the idea of leaving it out, but worried you wouldn't have anywhere to park, so in the garage it went. I opened the door from the garage to the house, and that was it. Out like a light. Black, black, and more black.

'I woke up with one of Steven's goons—what is it with bullies and their goons—slapping my face. They tied me to a bed. Nice touch. I asked where I was and what was going on. The goon said I'd find out in due course and slammed the door on his way out. I'm not easily frightened, but even I understood the gravity of my situation. There was no point yelling out or struggling—I'd already tried that. I was panicked, though. I think that's understandable.'

'How long were you in the bedroom?' Sandy asked.

'I honestly don't know. The curtains were closed; I could see the beginning and the end of each day. Three days, maybe? The room had an ensuite, so when I needed to go, they'd untie me and stand guard, then tie me up again. It was like something from a movie. I think I deserve an Oscar nomination, to be honest.'

'Just the facts, Brad,' Sandy snapped.

'They untied me and took me into the kitchen, where they forced me onto a chair. Then, lo-and-behold, my brother turns up. The brother my father told me to kill, who I didn't kill, whose death I fudged to fool my father. The brother who I spent hundreds of thousands of dollars on a new identity for, and relocated to Spain. It took a while for me to work out what was going on, to put it all together, to realise that Steven was the one pulling the strings. Literally. I felt quite guilty about all the things I'd said to and about my father. I also realised that the feeling of being watched at home was my brother's handiwork.

'He kept me there, in his house, for weeks. I got sick of trying to keep track. Each day ran into the other. I was a prisoner and treated like one. Two showers a week, no clean clothes, bland meals, no privacy, no sunshine. Steven wasn't there much; his goons did all the heavy lifting. When he made an appearance, it was to torment me emotionally and mentally. His goons did the physical tormenting. I think that's all now, Detective Sanderson. There's no more to tell. I'm finding it quite draining.'

I waited while Sandy stopped the recorder on his phone.

'Okay?' I asked him.

'Yes. Well done. I know it's hard. I think that will be enough. We can wrap up.'

Ebony, who had been sitting at the kitchen table pretending to work on her laptop, came over and sat next to me.

'If those men who pretended to work for your father hadn't had a change of heart, you wouldn't have made it out of your brother's clutches alive,' she said. She wiped her eyes.

I tried to lean in to kiss her cheek, but it hurt too much.

'Will I ever be able to go back to my Ebony Makepeace life?' she asked Sandy.

'No. Ebony Makepeace is dead. We had a funeral for her. Her Estate is wrapped up, her life assurance paid, her friends and parents are trying to move on. And Douglas Culley is suspected of her murder.'

'What's going to happen with Steven?' I asked Sandy.

'He's going away for a long time: kidnapping, false imprisonment, murder, extortion. I'm sure we will find something else.'

'I'm sure he'll find a way to get around it all,' I said, listening to the nasty sarcasm in my voice.

'And if he does, we won't be safe.' Ebony looked at me with the worried expression she wore the whole time I was trying to resettle her. It broke my heart. Something had to be done to make sure Steven was eliminated one way or another.

Ebony made the three of us a coffee, and she and Sandy sat at the kitchen table while I was in quarantine on the couch. She whipped up some sandwiches and brought me over a tomato, cheese, and lettuce one. I think

I'll have to get used to a no meat diet.

The things we do.

———

Sandy left a message to call him. Ebony and I had been—well— busy when he tried to reach me.

'What's happening?' I asked as soon as he answered.

'Steven got bail. Against our advice to the magistrate. We said he was a flight risk. Guess what? He's flown the coop.'

I said nothing. What was there to say? I hung up and walked over to Ebony who was sitting on the balcony going through those interminable notebooks.

She looked at me with those eyes that penetrated my being when I had something awful to say to her. It's like she knew without me even speaking.

'Now what?'

'Steven is on the run.'

'Are we leaving?' she asked without so much as a flinch.

'No. I'm going to find the prick. He knows what happened to my mother...'

(TO BE CONTINUED...)

ABOUT THE AUTHOR

Janeen Ann O'Connell was born and grew up in Melbourne, Victoria, Australia. Her parents separated before her first birthday, and her maternal grandmother had primary care of Janeen until she was six. It was her grandmother's strong sense of justice, her strong political will, and the passion filled stories she told of her childhood and the Depression years, that instilled a love of family history and politics into the aspiring writer. It was during her family history research that Janeen learned her grandmother's cousin was Premier of the State of Victoria from 1924 until 1927 and her uncle was a mayor and councillor in regional Victoria. Janeen now understood where her interest in politics came from.

Her family history has lots more secrets, adventures, political misadventures, pioneer challenges, insane asylum admissions, bankruptcies and happy stories to share. Janeen lives in a suburb of Melbourne, Victoria, Australia with her husband and their miniature poodle, Teddy. She has two daughters, one son, four granddaughters and one grandson.

To learn more about Janeen Ann O'Connell and discover more Next Chapter authors, visit our website at www.nextchapter.pub.

Ebony Makepeace is Dead
ISBN: 978-4-82414-204-7
Mass Market

Published by
Next Chapter
2-5-6 SANNO
SANNO BRIDGE
143-0023 Ota-Ku, Tokyo
+818035793528

2nd April 2022

www.ingramcontent.com/pod-product-compliance
Lightning Source LLC
LaVergne TN
LVHW031238190726
843491LV00012B/3034